INTO IT

Edward Pomerantz

toExcel
San Jose New York Lincoln Shanghai

Into It

All Rights Reserved. Copyright © 1972, 2000 by Edward Pomerantz

No part of this book may be reproduced or transmitted in any form or by any means, graphic, electronic, or mechanical, including photocopying, recording, taping, or by any information storage or retrieval system, without the permission in writing from the publisher.

Published by toExcel Press,
an imprint of iUniverse.com, Inc.

For information address:
iUniverse.com, Inc.
620 North 48th Street
Suite 201
Lincoln, NE 68504-3467
www.iuniverse.com

ISBN: 0-595-09132-6

For Sandy Kazan
our children
Francesca and Alexandra
and for
Gert and Al Pomerantz
my mother and father

I write of the wish that comes true . . . the wish with terror in it . . .

—James M. Cain

ONE

1

I'm into it now. Tell me this is the way it would go two months ago and I'd have told you you were seeing too many movies, reading too many books. But then who'd believe those mothers-for-peace on television last week—run down by tanks. Or your father dying of a heart attack one night: running in to find him backing out of your mother, still erect, begging you to cover him, even in pain. Is that what this is all about? Two ordinary people. Somebody *else's* mother and father and here I am on my back waiting for the mother to make a meal of me again—all fifty ordinary years of her—while the father, Joe, is on *his* back—in the hospital—all beat up and ordinary.

It's amazing the way you get into things. I was standing on the street corner waiting for the light to change, only instead of going back upstairs with the cigarettes and club soda for my mother's wedding, I kept walking—I didn't even have my wallet or keys, just the change from the cigarettes—straight to the movies where I don't remember what I saw, I just kept listening to my heart pumping through six shows and inside the john where I stood on the toilet until it was safe to come out.

If you really want to pass the survival test, try waking up in an old movie lounge under a framed *Photoplay* cover of somebody called Alice Faye. If that and warm Canada Dry and Salems for breakfast don't send you home, nothing will. Not even guilt, which I blew my last buck on with a telegram saying Forgive Me. I still don't know what I had in mind or what I would have done next. The first time you're down to your last nickel all you can think of is starving to death. But you don't starve. You wait. Some meals take longer than others.

Like lunch. Call it beginners' luck, but there I am in the supermarket lined up with my nickel's worth of gum when this blonde in front of me with two big bundles drops a barbecued chicken on my foot and I offer to help her home.

I don't usually give my delivery boys such a big tip, she says later, yanking the drumstick out from under her. Generosity is its own reward, I mumble, nibbling at the wish. That's when she tells me about her husband and how he never gets off the phone. How even in the middle of doing it, he always takes a call. Just in case there's another deal, another million on the other end. Then she laughs and then she cries. And then she tells me how one night he picked it up, only it was for *her* this time, so he kept right on going, while her sister was telling her, faster, harder, about her mother, right over the edge, who was dead.

It's amazing the things they tell you afterward. Especially strangers.

Then she jumps out of bed and says okay, now get the hell out of here and don't touch my valuables. I had no intention of touching her valuables so when she goes into the bathroom I take her slipper, her ballpoint and her portable Sony.

Which is how I got into this.

I had to duck in somewhere when I saw the cop.

"Sorry, we're closing," the small redheaded lady in the mackinaw and Mammy Yokum boots tells me, puffing on a Tiparillo and taking off her apron, the pocket stitched Mrs. Joe.

"I'll take anything you have," I tell her, putting the TV down, out of sight of the window, the cop looking in.

"Not a piece of fish left. Not even the ice."

A big guy around sixty with a Smoky The Bear hat and a red bandana around his neck comes out of the toilet and goes to the sink, turning the faucets on full steam, scraping his board clean of blood.

"Could I have a glass of water?"

The cop goes by and I collapse to the stool.

"Of course. What's the matter with you?"

"Nothing. I'm fine."

"You look terrible." She puts out the cigar.

"I don't have any money. I was on my way to the pawnshop to hock the TV when I got dizzy. I thought I'd leave the set here in return for some fish."

"Don't be ridiculous. Joe, the boy is sick."

The big guy comes over and puts his wet smelly hands on me. "Where do you live?"

"I've been kicked out. Look, I'm sorry. I didn't mean to burden you."

"Joe, let's drive him to the hospital."

"No, please. I'm okay. All I need is some supper . . ."

"The Salvation Army's on the way downtown."

"He can't stand on line," she says. "They'll give him soup."

"What should I do?" he says. "Take him home with us?"

2

Over supper, she got the helper idea.

"How do you know he wants a job?" He sits there naked except for a wraparound terry, blubber-bellied, nipples like dots.

"Of course he wants one. He's gotta eat, don't he?"

She's in a kimono with pom-pom slip-ons.

"He's doing all right."

He points his fork at my plate: Pot roast and noodles. Veal parmigian.

He laughs. I laugh. She lights a cigar.

"You got a mother and father?"

"My father's dead. My mother's married again."

"Oh," she says. "We got a son. Only he doesn't live here. He lives out west. Maybe you saw him. He was on the Tonight Show twice."

"What's his name?"

"Danny Dime. That's his stage name, of course. He used to be an English professor."

"Instructor," Joe says.

"What's the difference? He teamed up with this other professor to write skits and before you know it they were doing it on television."

I soak my bread in the gravy.

"Where's he now? Hollywood?"

Joe laughs: "Not quite."

"Texas," she says, eyeing him down. "He was in the middle of this tour playing colleges all over the country, on the way to Vegas, as a matter of fact, when that no-good Nichols, that was his partner . . . Nichols and Dime, get it? They really could have made it. I told Danny not to take any wooden nickels. Joe says he gets most of his material from me. What do you need Nichols for, I said. It's *your* jokes they're laughing at. And sure enough, what do you think Nichols goes and does?"

"What?"

"Gets a phone call. From California. This movie producer he knows—that's how you get these things—says Drop Everything and write this movie for me—leaving Danny you know where—as *he* says, up the creek on the Mexican border in a motel room watching *Run For Your Life.*"

"You sound just like him," Joe says.

"Well, I've listened to him tell it often enough.

When he went on tour, we bought him this portable tape recorder—I knew he'd never *write* us—then November when the baby was born we sent him this *video*-tape machine. Have you ever seen one? It's better than movies. You just plug it into the TV and keep playing it over and over. After supper, I'll show you."

"What does he want to see Danny and the baby for?" Joe asks, annoyed.

"Why not? The baby's adorable. Looks just like Amy—with Danny's nose. That's why Amy married him, Danny says." Doing an imitation: "Dumb confederate. She never saw a nose like it before." She laughs. "As luck would have it, the night Nichols ran out, she went up to Danny for his autograph and they were married a week later. For Amy's graduation. I can't say I was exactly ecstatic about it, but if you really want to know, it couldn't have worked out better. Amy teaching these poor Mexican and Indian kids. Danny home every day. Working on his single."

"I should have such luck," Joe says.

"You're not in show business. Besides, what would you do with yourself all day? He's away from the store an hour, you never saw a crazier man. He's got diabetes. And heart failure into the bargain. The doctor warned him: At your age, if you don't cut down and get some help you can go just like that." She snaps her fingers.

"We can *all* go like that." He snaps his.

"My brother Sam went like that." She snaps. "But he *lived*. He *went* places."

"I'll take you places," Joe says. "Get up at five in the morning tomorrow, I'll take you to the Fulton Fish Market."

"Take *him*." She points at me, my mouth full of pot roast. I stop chewing.

He looks me over.

"You believe in work? Or you just hock things?"

I swallow: "Sure."

"Sure what?"

"Sure I've worked."

"Doing what?"

"Lifeguard. The docks."

"What do you mean the docks?"

"I unload at night sometimes. When you don't have to be union."

He tries not to look impressed. Then: "What about school?"

"What about it?"

"You're only a kid. You go, don't you?"

"I'm twenty-two. And I quit."

"What's the matter? No ambition? Or your mother ran out of money?"

"I was paying for it myself. And it stopped making sense. Maybe some other time it will."

"Won't they draft you?"

"They have to find me first."

"But that's breaking the law," she says.
"I wouldn't go, anyway."
"What are you? A hippie?" he says.
"What do I look like?"
He goes back to his noodles.
"Isn't your mother worried?"
"She's got somebody."
Him again: "What did your father do?"
"He was a painter."
"Of what? Pictures or houses?"
"Pictures."
"Did he make a living?"
"Sometimes."
He soaks his bread: "I used to paint."
She laughs.
He stares her down. "I used to pose, too."
"For what? Whale posters?"
"I didn't always look like this. Only after I married you."
She lets that one go.
"I don't blame you for leaving school," she says, "with what's going on."
"I just needed time out," I tell her.
"Time out for what?" he says.
"For whatever happens."
He smiles: "Working in a fish store?"
"Maybe."
"And what happens when you get the itch again . . . when you need time out?"

"What do you want," she says, "a lifetime contract?"

"Like everybody else, he probably thinks fish stinks."

"It doesn't? Treat him human, he might surprise you."

"Nobody wants to work anymore, not even the colored, the Puerto Rican."

"Some of us got no choice," she says. Then a fast one to me: "Seventy-five dollars a week with tips for deliveries."

He almost chokes: "Are you crazy?"

"And all the free fish you can eat."

"My wife is crazy. You'll have to forgive her."

To her again: "Who died and left *you* in charge?"

"You wanna *keep* a man? *Pay* him."

"This is no A and P. It's a *personality* business. People don't want to do trade with strangers. A customer walks in, you gotta know how to talk to him, open a clam . . ."

"Teach him. Like you taught me."

"I don't have another lifetime."

They give each other the look again. She gets up. "What do you want for dessert? Dietetic or regular?"

"A little of each."

She laughs, in spite of herself, puts out her cigar, and goes to the refrigerator.

"You'll like it with us," she says. "I guarantee it.

The smell—forget about. Live as long as I have, you get used to it. At night, you can soak it off."

"That smell puts food on this table," he says.

"All right, don't excite yourself."

"That smell paid for your son's college education so he could live off a wife."

He must be wearing a flameproof vest because the look she gives him now can burn a hole right through him. He looks at me, embarrassed, then down at his hands. We sit there without saying anything while she scoops out the ice cream. Then after we're finished, he says, "My wife's mouth is bigger than her pocketbook. If I offered you sixty, would you take it?"

I'm not sure I want it, so I don't answer.

"You could stay here," she says, "till you find a place."

This time he *does* choke.

"Why not?" she says. "The room is empty, isn't it? It used to be Danny's. Why should you pay rent?"

I look at Joe.

"It's *yours*," she says, "if you take the job."

In my coat all I have is the slipper and the ballpoint. The TV is hockable, but not tonight. And outside, it's the end of February.

"*You're* the boss," I say, to Joe.

3

After the dishes, I made a tour of my room. Joe was asleep by 8:15. "The alarm goes off at four thirty. Don't stay up all night watching Danny."

Mrs. Joe was in the bath, soaking.

Reading the walls, I found him everywhere: Pictures, plaques, two-dollar mother's day cards, satin-heart valentines, army discharge, straight-A report cards, diplomas, wedding invitation, birth announcements—his own, his baby's—news clippings, reviews, underlined TV schedules. Everything out. Not even framed. Just thumbtacked or scotch-taped like bandages trying to catch up with an exploding skin. It made me itch. I wanted to turn everything over, sure I'd find the exact opposite on the other side: bloated babies instead of adorable birthday boys, skulls for faces, straight F's, obituaries. On the windowsill, a bronze cup from Camp Totona. For Character and Swimming. Inside, dead bugs.

What I couldn't figure out was who or what he was. In the beginning, a fat little kid, then skinny, then fat, then skinny again. You couldn't tell if he was good-looking or not, he was one of these personality kids, no sex, just smile, the kind who learns what hustling is early, only he doesn't know it's hustling till it's too late and people aren't buying anymore. This kid was selling Bounce, popular with widows, grandmothers, cock-scared schoolteachers. Just pinch my cheek and I'll Pledge Allegiance for you. Instant Promise. Fulfilled on the spot. No sweat, no stink. Just stand in my light. According to the pictures, the light was on all the time. Or at least every time he knew you were snapping his picture. That was the problem. Without *you,* he had no switch.

The switch, as a kid, was obviously Mama, pretty and sexy in her pin-up girl bathing suit, cheek-to-cheeking it with her little prince, while Papa, with hair then, hung and handsome, held a handful of tit, tongueing her nipple, doing his Groucho for the gang at the beach. Moving along—more cheek-to-cheeking—in graduation gowns, on dance floors, in front of national monuments. Papa, greying, balding, fattening, while Mama turns to leather, toughens, creases, face and body—forming a fist.

"That was us at Niagara Falls."

Before I turn around, I can smell her behind me. Perfumed bouillabaise. Steamed and smothered.

"Danny was eighteen there. Just before he left for college. That's how long it's been since I've gone on a trip."

She's toweling her hair in an orange terry. I can see freckles at the tops of her breasts. Her bare feet are boiled-red, her chipped red toenails need a once-over.

"I'll play just one so you can get some sleep." She goes to the machine and threads a tape. "This was the first. Right after the baby was born." She turns on the TV. "Put out the light."

I flick the switch and Danny Dime comes on.

"Hello, you lucky people . . ."

She laughs and sits next to me on the convertible sofa.

"What a toy . . ."

He looks like his pictures, the short skinny ones. Still a kid, only his hair's not exactly there anymore.

"Leave it to you, Ma, to make a public spectacle of me . . . What do you want to see first? . . . The bathroom? The refrigerator?" He does the salesman bit, opening and closing the refrigerator in a flash, without showing us anything.

"Just like you thought. Empty. She's starving me to death." She throws her head back and giggles, reaching for her cigars. I hand them to her, but it's like I'm no longer there. "As a matter of fact, I expect her home any minute. With the paycheck. In the meantime, this might be of interest to you . . ." He holds up a baby. "Your grandson."

She blows out a match, aaahs, throws kisses.

"Say something, stupid. Your grandfather didn't spend all this money so he could watch you sleep. I don't know what's the matter with him. He was up two days ago. That's how long it took me to figure out how to work this thing . . . Speak, dummy, speak . . ."

The baby starts to cry.

"Oh, for Christ's sake . . ."

He backs away and dumps the baby in the crib.

"Will you look at what he did to me? And that wasn't even rehearsed."

She's laughing so hard now, she chokes on smoke.

"Amy? Is that you?"

All of a sudden there's a blur.

"Wait a minute. Don't come in yet."

More blurring and noise, then a girl comes on, carrying a load of groceries, blonde and pretty, around twenty-three.

"Don't look now. But you're on Candid Camera."

She looks bewildered, tries to smile, the baby's screaming now, she puts down the bundles.

"Just be natural. Say hello to the folks."

"He's soaking wet," she says. "Why didn't you change him?"

"You're Doris Day, remember? Not Anna Magnani. Now say hello and we'll fight later."

She looks at the camera, confused, angry. "Hello, Mom. Hello, Dad." Then to Danny: "Turn it off."

"Oh, shit. Just get out of the way."

She reacts like he's slapped her, on the verge of tears.

He comes in the picture and stands in front of her. "It's *I Love Lucy,* folks. What they never show you."

She picks up the baby and goes away.

"Just a typical day in the life of a typical couple. Fibber McGee and Dopey. Raskolnikov and Gracie."

A plane flying low drowns him out. The picture shakes and he holds his ears.

"Nothing to be alarmed about. We're just being invaded. One of life's little bonuses when you're stranded in an army town. Have you heard the latest? We're at war down here. Just a game they call it—Organization Cleansweep—to prepare our Reserves for the real thing, reassure the country we can meet any emergency—no bodies or anything, at least not yet—but the whole town's involved. They've even taken some of Amy's Mexican and Indian kids and put them in 'strategic hamlets' where she's supposed to convert them to the American Way of Life. Oh, well . . . In the meantime, how would you like your money's worth? That's right, you lucky people. For the first time ever—on house-to-house video—that star of stage, screen, and his mother's wallpaper

—brought to you live from thirty-one record-breaking years at your neighborhood Loews—the one and only Danny Dime—*In* Poysen. . . ."

He Durantes off and right back on again.

"Hi. I wonder if you have the same problem *I* have—this terrific pressure to be happy all the time. You know what I mean? I know it's my right. That I'm *supposed* to be happy. But when I'm not, is that any reason why I should feel guilty? How do we even know happiness exists? You figure there's an *un*happy, there's gotta be a happy, right? But where is it? I mean, like everybody's right and nobody's happy. Have you noticed? Somewhere along the way somebody held up this sign: To Happy. And even though you listened and paid attention and made all the right turns, you ended up—in Canarsie . . ."

She cracks up here.

"Tell the truth. Are *you* happy? Or are you just like I am? . . ."

"Over thirty and confused." She gives the answer before he does. He stops and smiles.

"That's the opening. You like it? I'm a little worried about the Canarsie—too New York, too ethnic, you know what I mean? I want it to be more universal, but it's gotta be personal, human at the same time. Without getting cute, sentimental . . . Like I've got this whole thing on what it's like to be short —how no matter how grown up you get, if you were ever a short or fat or skinny kid, that's *it*—how the mirror reads—for the rest of your life. I still remember how humiliating it was every time a teacher said: All right, everybody, line up in size place . . . and the whole class stepped aside for me. Or my cousin Jumbo—every time we'd get in a car—it was always: Jumbo, *you* sit up front with the men. Danny, *you* back here—on Aunt Sophie's lap. The only time being short had any advantage was in Music Appreciation when I threw up on Michael Proctor sitting *in front of* me and he turned around and socked Cookie Silverbush sitting *behind* me. Get the picture? . . .

"There's this G.I. coffeehouse in town—lets me have the floor on Friday nights so I can try the stuff out. I spoke to Bernie, my agent, he said he'd fly out here or send one of his representatives soon as I had something in shape. He doesn't have to now. I can send him a tape. Who knows, you lucky people, the prodigal son's return may be sooner than you think . . ."

He flicks an imaginary cigar and does the Groucho eyebrow bit.

"Well, look who's back."

Amy and the baby again, the baby all dolled up and pacified now, Amy with her hair combed, pinned back. She smiles.

"There's my girl."

He kisses her.

"And Little Lord Fauntleroy, too."

He plays with a toe. Then: "Amy's a little upset these days because her mother has to go into the hospital next week. Nothing serious or anything. Just a checkup."

Another plane flies low and they huddle together.

"We're a little late, folks . . ."

The baby screams.

"This is where you came in . . ."

He comes forward and blacks out the screen.

She gets up and turns it off.

"There's more but we'll save it. I don't want to throw too much at you all at once. Wait till you see what he does with my brother Marty. He has him down to a tee. What do you sleep in? Pajamas or shorts?"

"Nothing."

"I'll give you a robe."

She goes to the closet and takes out a kimono. "You'll need warm clothes. The market is freezing. There's some long underwear of Danny's here—he never wore. And put on these galoshes. I don't want you catching pneumonia."

I get up and start pulling out the sofa.

"The sheet is clean. Nobody's slept on it since Danny."

She gives me a blanket from the top of the closet.

"I leave the bathroom light on for Joe. With

diabetes, you get up at night. If you can't sleep, just shut the door."

"Thanks. I really appreciate it."

"Stick *with* it, we'll treat you like our own." She stands there for a minute, then shrugs and smiles. "Good night," she says. "I left you a toothbrush on the sink."

The bathroom smells like she does, the walls are a drugstore's. A shelf for her—of atomizers, powders, sachets, deodorizers. Another for him—of bay rum, witch hazel, Old Spice, Canoe. In each corner of the tub a large open clam shell, one with cigar butts, the others with soaps—little limes, lemons, oranges, strawberries.

I get into bed, stinking Danny out.

4

Four thirty. Right on the nose.

A cold hand shakes me awake.

"Hurry up," he says. "I'll meet you downstairs."

His urine is in the toilet, I flush it down with my own, thinking of my father, his persistent dick, peeing and coming at the instant of death.

Outside, the night is an icy slate, sharpening your eyes into steel knives. He's sitting in the station wagon, heat on full mixed with years of fish. He puts on the radio, we don't speak, we slide down the Drive, its only riders, toward the Brooklyn Bridge frozen in ink, then under the Drive and along the docks till we come to the market like into a dream.

There's no way to tell it—go for yourself—this

gushing frontier of wet and flesh, this predawn nighttown that lives in your sleep.

We park and get out, but I can't keep up as he glides ahead along the movie-set streets through fluorescent drizzle past stalls like sea caves down sidewalks like streams around trucks behind lifts between tattooed muscles, fucken motherfuckers, giant swordfish hanging over in scales—headless, slit open, into giant cunt—past a Chinese lady with a flowered umbrella, a skull-capped Jew, squirming lobsters.

I catch up at a stall where he's yelling his order. The bookkeeper, in a cage, taps his window: "Hey, Joe. Is that your son?"

"New man," he shouts back. "I'm breaking him in."

"Wait here," he says to me, "while I take a shit."

Inside it feels like an underwater operating room, a subterranean factory for all-night surgery. Cold steam rises from the slatted floor gripping your groin with an icy hand as rubber-aproned men in high rubber boots with red-trimmed grey socks and yellow caps stand at running faucets and knife-scraped flounder boards under rosebud-nippled women with balloon breasts who wink at them from calendars in various positions as they slice, rip, discard skin into barrels, lay the meat in tins, while others string bass through scooped-out eyeballs, sloshing them in kegs of bloodied water that flows endlessly down gutters into slurping drains.

He comes out and I follow him to breakfast in a corner saloon next to a walk-up hotel with a Bowery staircase, empty overhead rooms. The saloon is divided into a bar and food counter. We sit at the counter in front of steaming corned beef, soups, hot cereals, sizzling eggs.

"For some people, this is supper. They've been up all night." He points to a table, two men drinking beer with whiskey chasers, eating mashed potatoes with gravy, steak, pea soup, rice pudding, pie.

He orders coffee, prunes, oatmeal, three fried— turned over.

Except for the prunes, I order the same. Mashed or french fries come with the eggs. I ask for hashbrown.

"Where do you think you are? The Plaza?"

Five minutes, we're finished, he pays my check.

"I'll deduct your food the end of the week. In the meantime, here's five. You shouldn't walk around without money."

We race across the cobblestone and back to the station wagon where they're loading his fish in baskets and tins.

"If you're too cold, wait in the car."

I can't feel my toes, but I stay where I am.

It's getting lighter. The night lifts. Sea caves

change to shanties with dripping roofs. Twinkling backdrop skyscrapers become concrete. What appeared from the distance to be a ghostly encampment is a huge open market with fires in garbage cans. I warm my ears and he yells come on. Back up the Drive and across to the store where he gives me gloves like hockey mitts and says start unloading. The halibut's frozen and weighs a ton. He shovels ice from a freezer into the showcase and window, I dump the halibut down and fall on top of it. Then I bring in the rest, everything icy. The gloves soak through, stick to the tins. I take them off, a fin cuts my finger. I drop a cod on the sidewalk, pick it up by its tail. It keeps slipping, he comes out with a hook. When I'm all finished, we load the case. My fingers won't bend, though, I can't open the tins. He says stand by the heater till you thaw out. I watch him as he works, swiftly, precisely, dumping fish out of baskets, then arranging them in rows, according to size. His hands move like a card shark's —dealing a fast one. I ask what each fish is, he answers: "Later." First, there are deliveries to bars and restaurants. He weighs shrimp, lobsters, filets, scallops, packs and marks them, tells me where to go.

"Blarney Stone'll give you coffee. Bring back donuts."

The bars stink from ammonia. There's no business. Just Puerto Ricans mopping, chairs on tables, Bugs Bunny, Hugh Downs playing to one or two drunks. I leave the fish in the kitchens and stop for the donuts and come back with my hands embracing the coffee.

A little Japanese man is waiting and smiling while Joe weighs a fish and wraps it as is.

The man pays and leaves.

"That's Mr. Azumo. He's here every morning at seven thirty. Always takes a porgy. Cleans it himself."

The store is quiet now. I realize how neat it is. Fishnet ceiling strung with cork floaters, swept sawdust floor, scrubbed tile walls. The first dollar, scotch-taped and scaled, above anchors, buoys, lobster ashtrays. The window's got a frame of little yellow fish —pointy the way a kid would paint them—around a hand-printed sign: JOE'S SEAFOOD GIVES YOU BRAINS. FREE DELIVERY. NO CHOLESTEROL.

Other customers straggle in ordering fish for later on their way home from work. A maid calls for shrimp, cooked and cleaned. He boils and salts the water in an empty filet tin. The first thing he teaches me is how to shell and devein them, pulling and picking in two quick steps. His fingers do their dealing like mechanical butterflies as he stands there and talks, rattling off each fish:

"The shiny blue is mackerel, the long pointy one is Spanish. The way you remember them is you can't see their scales. They're smooth and slippery. Not like pike. The pike is the yellow, watch out they don't stick you. The big one is carp, only moves on holidays. The Jews make gefilte fish with it, the Gentiles save the scales. Don't ask me why, it's supposed to bring luck. Over there is striped bass. Beauties, every one of them. Red snapper. Smelts. Soft-shells. Piss-clams. Halibut, you know. The salmon is frozen; don't say so unless they ask. Crab meat is in the icebox, six-fifty a pound. . . ."

A woman comes in in rags and dirty feet. He gives her cod necks and tails and takes a dime as she bows and blesses us in the name of her cats.

"Cats, my ass. She's got soup for a week now."

More phone calls, customers, I make my first sale. He watches from his board as I go to the register, says good-bye and thank you for me, and goes on with his boning.

"Shad," he says. "They're just starting to come in."

I go over and watch as he slits the silver belly, moves his hand inside, gently probing, and scoops out a roe, plump and scarlet, like a heart.

He talks as he works, fast and happy.

"Their season starts in February, ends in May. I used to make my living in those four months just boning shad every morning from three to eleven for the wholesalers, the restaurants. The shad's in the herring family, got a thousand bones, like little needles, sixty to a mouthful. Before *me,* you couldn't eat them. Indians used to grab them out of the river with their bare hands, then smoke and bury them and live on them for a year. *We* used them for fertilizer or cooked them for five hours. What a shame, I thought. Their meat is delicious. Rich and moist. Why turn them to mush?"

The shad in front of him lies split, intact. He runs his knife along one side and unzips a tiny comb of curved bones with a long tweezer.

"So I got this idea. I was helping out a cousin in his fish store in Philadelphia. No job, a family, the middle of the Depression. I was glad to do it, especially the shad. If I could just get at those bones, underneath all those layers. You can't even see them and they run a million directions. I brought one shad to a doctor and said X-ray this, will you? That's when I got the idea of the tweezer. My first shad took three hours. I left a mess and no fish. Then, an hour and a half, pretty soon—eight minutes. I still tell my customers I'll pay them a quarter if they can find a bone, or any of their fish on my knife."

Inserting his thumb, he massages a groove.

"I finally got it down to a minute and a half. That's when I went to the restaurants with a printed card saying Professional Shad Boner. You should have seen me—just like a surgeon—with a black satchel, rubber gloves, white apron, knife and tweezer. You think my son's a showman? I had chefs and waiters stopping their work at Lindy's, Paddy's, Gage and Tollner. Fish experts from all over the world came to see how I did it. They left with their heads shaking. I was too fast for them. Paddy finally put me in the window with a big hat catching the crowds on their way to Macy's, out of Pennsylvania Station. The Army wouldn't take me 'cause I was *one of a kind*. Without *me,* America would choke to death."

He laughs.

"Like everything else, it's a gimmick. A gimmick and an art. See those nails? Filed and manicured. To keep the fingers light. The lighter they are, the faster they work. If I didn't get sick, I'd still only bone shad. . . . Who wants to work from five in the morning to six at night every day? My wife's got it all wrong. I used to finish Lindy's at eleven thirty and be in the Roxy by twelve. I could've even had a studio and had time to paint, if nobody laughed. Who needs a store? During the war, I had a chance to go in on a big seafood restaurant in Provincetown, the wop who owns it made a fortune. But you think he's free? His daughter just ran away with a black busboy and he's never had a Sunday off."

He finishes the fish and folds it together again.

"Not *me.* One thing I could never do was work for anybody. I always had to be in business for myself."

He washes the shad and tells me to lay it in the window on the ice.

"If there's one thing I can't stand it's getting paid

what everybody else is getting. That's why I'm against Unions. Even if I end up making less, it's *me* who determines what I'm worth. Nobody else . . ."

I come back and he starts on another.

"Now you wanna learn something?"

Mrs. Joe comes in and says oh my God.

We look up.

"What's the matter?"

"Will you look at his feet? They're drenched. Right through his socks." She's lifting my pants. "Why didn't you take the galoshes?"

"Leave him alone."

"They were too small," I tell her.

"Take off your shoes. I'll go across to Woolworth's and buy slippers. What's your size? I'll get galoshes, too."

Before we can stop her, she's out the door.

I shrug and laugh. Joe shakes his head, picks up a scissor and goes on with my lesson.

"The first thing you do on any fish is snip the fins off." He snips, then scrapes, and picks up his knife.

"When you're cutting off the head, it's straight across at the neck. Then you cut the tail off up here, getting rid of all the bones down there. Now you're ready to slit it. Make sure it's facing you . . . and run the knife very slowly down to here where the intestinal hole is, you don't want to rip the roe, they're two-fifty a pair. . . ."

He runs the blade inside and with his other hand cleans out the guts.

Then, once again, the roe, plump and scarlet, like before. He holds it out to me, enjoying its feel, its weight. "Just like a baby. Inside the woman. The buck shad are smaller, they've got narrower bellies. All the female strength is in these little beads, thousands of eggs wrapped in membrane, just like cellophane, go ahead and feel it. . . ."

Wet and adhesive, it sticks to my fingers.

"Protected by three layers of bones and they're still not safe. If *we* don't catch them, the flies get them—when the mamas swim upstream in pairs to spawn."

He lets me take it.

"The ones that escape swim out to sea but they always come back to the river they were born in."

A teacher I had once said I had a nose for metaphor. He should have seen me now—one sitting in my hand.

"Nobody knows where the shad comes from. They're all over. Florida. New Orleans. The Carolinas. Maine. The ones in the Mississippi they call mud or stink shad. Even the Hudson shad—you can smell the sewerage, the oil from tankers. These are Connecticut River. You wanna see the nets? We'll take a ride one Sunday. They can't be caught with bait, see? They have no teeth. . . ."

He opens the mouth of the cut-off head. Mrs. Joe comes back with an overstuffed shopping bag.

"Everything is stretch—one size fits all."

She takes out socks, Totes, gloves, ear muffs.

"Where did you shop?" he asks. "The five-and-ten in Alaska?"

"Try these on," she says. "They don't fit, I'll return them." She gives me desert boots with pile lining.

"These are expensive."

She shrugs: "Thom McAn."

Joe looks at her, shakes his head again.

"How's he doing?" she asks him. "Has he learned to bone a shad yet?"

"I was just teaching him. Before the fashion show."

"It takes a couple of years. You think you'll be with us?"

I smile and take my shoes off. She goes to where the phone is. A shelf with a stool, adding machine, pads. A mirror trimmed with snapshots of Danny and the baby.

"Mrs. Arlen was supposed to go out at nine," she says. "What's her order still doing here?"

"Did you leave the slip where I would find it?" he asks her.

"I told you last night." This time *she* shakes it. "It never fails. If I don't do it myself. . . ."

"Try coming in on time."

"I wanted to give you a chance. To see what it was like—*without* me."

"They fit," I tell her. I'm wearing the boots and socks.

"Run this out for me, will you? She's one of our biggest customers."

I take the order and bike to Park Avenue. Two doors down from the lady with the valuables. Only this time the doorman won't let me up. Around the back, he says, where I get a nickel tip.

The rest of the day is odds and ends. Sweeping, shoveling, hosing down the ice. Mrs. Joe—on her stool, puffing away, giving out recipes, taking cash, exchanging snapshots of babies with grandmother customers, handing out lollipops to kids in carriages, rolling filet around salmon, frying flounder for our lunch, running out for hot chocolate, danish, seeded rolls.

Around five thirty, I pick a shad up myself, run my hand along its back, smell my fingers. Joe catches me pantomiming his act.

"You wanna practice? Start with porgies. They're only thirty-nine cents a pound." He takes the knife away. "In the meantime, *watch*."

He performs the ritual: the beheading, the abortion. Then he splits the fish down the middle and opens it up, laying it flat and removing the spine. Then he runs the blade up under the bones and turns the knife around to lift them out and away.

"There are sixty rib bones on each side." He goes under after them, making cuts, switching knife for tweezer, leaving boneless grooves. Then he puts his finger in to lift the meat away from a *second* layer of sixty *more* bones which he tweezes out a few at a time. Then the whole thing repeated on the other side, his thumbs and fingers inserting, massaging, disappearing inside each groove, until the fish lies there, like twin vaginas, each fleshy and hilly, in its multiple folds.

"Time to ice up," she says. "It's six o'clock."

We ice the unsold fish, make a last-minute sale.

"Bundle up," she says. "It's starting to snow."

We huddle in the station wagon three in front and listen to the news to get the weather. Up the West Side Highway past an aircraft carrier, the Hudson, like an ocean, bleak and angry. In front of the house, she gets out of the car.

"You and Joe go upstairs," I say. "*I'll* park."

"Go on. Get out of here."

"It's freezing," I tell him.

"I froze *before* you. I'll freeze *after* you."

"You can *both* freeze," she says. And slams the door.

We ride around the block to an underground parking lot, then race across a playground back to the house. Upstairs, she's ecstatic, a new tape from Danny. Any bills, he asks. And soaks his feet. Dinner, he's quiet. Just her—all excited, laughing in advance at Danny's jokes. Then right after coffee: "Good night," he says.

"Aren't you going to watch?"

"I'm too tired. Watch it with Nick. I'll see it tomorrow."

He goes into the bedroom, she flings down a spoon.

"His own son and he's too tired."

For the first time, he's called me by name.

5

"Hello, you lucky people. I've got good news and bad news . . ."

We've taken our seats, both bathed and robed, eating chocolate ice cream in our lobster feet.

"First, the bad news. Bernie turned me down. Said the act was terrific but he couldn't peddle it. Too Henny Youngman, what they want now is blue stuff. . . . I tell you, with this new permissiveness there isn't anything you can't do anymore. Just this morning I got an ad in the mail for a new penis. Right away, I think: Who put me on the mailing list? . . . Guaranteed satisfaction or your money back. . . . Keep the money, just return the old one . . . No operation necessary. Just slip it on . . . If it can slip *on,* it can slip *off* . . . One size fits all

. . . Then how will the Prince know it was *me* at the Ball last night and not my wicked step-sisters? . . . Comes in black and white . . . Well, Amos, what do you think of old Andy now? . . . State religious preference . . . One Moslem, clipped . . ."

We're both laughing. She slaps my thigh.

"Things are getting so bad, I can't even make love to my wife without the latest x-rated movie running through my head. The other night I was kissing close-ups, flash-cuts, zoomed-in belly-button. Speaking of x-rated movies, I've thought of a great way to end the war: No one under twenty-one allowed to go unless accompanied by an adult . . . I tried that out at the G.I. coffeehouse on Friday, they went wild for it . . . Which reminds me of the *good* news. Just in case you were beginning to think I was a bum or something, I've taken a job. Nothing nine to five or anything, actually I'm in business for myself. At least, it *looks* that way. It's really a front. What I mean is the FBI or the CIA, they can't tell *themselves* apart, why should I? . . . anyhow, one of their henchmen knocked on my door the other day and put up the money for me to run this employment agency—servicing enlisted men and their wives with domestics and caddies. It seems they caught my act at this anti-war coffeehouse one night and with Amy teaching these Chicano and Indian kids, they figured I'd be the last person anybody would suspect of working for the Central Intelligence Agency. The whole thing is harmless, which is the only reason I took the stupid thing, not to mention the monthly grand I get. All I have to do is keep my eyes and ears open, as they say, and they really *do* say things like that, to find out if any of my caddies and babysitters—a lot of these Chicano and Indian kids—are being propositioned or screwed by any of the officers or their wives. Homosexual officers and nymphomaniac wives aren't exactly known for keeping their mouths shut, you might say, especially when they're being blackmailed into giving out top-secret information. And if you remember correctly, there's a 'war' going on here, which has had its run extended. It was supposed to only run two months, but with unemployment going up and with the latest bombing, riot, and massacre threats, they gotta do something to keep the kids off the streets, so instead of concentration camps they keep drafting them and sending them down here. Which is just God's way of blessing this town—as one of our local merchants put it—there isn't anybody who isn't making a profit. You can buy bows and arrows, watches, 'happy cigarettes,' right off the sidewalk. The only hitch is our little war exercise is beginning to get real. The other day some gas escaped from a low-flying plane which the Army assured was only harmful to crops. Nothing to panic about, folks, they told us on local television, the most it can cause is a slight virus. Well, you never saw such a mess. People running wild. In and out of bathrooms, bushes, outhouses. Doing it in buckets, wells, hats. Horses groaning. Cows keeling over. Birds shrieking, flapping, splattering. I got these great tapes—of people running for cover, a squadron of pigeons coming out of the clouds, soldiers jumping in foxholes, grabbing for helmets, guns . . . Who knows? Maybe I'll get a movie out of this . . . In the meantime, I'm taking your advice, Dad. Always have a little something on the side. A little gimmick or racket, you used to call it. Well, how about pimping and spying? Is that what you had in mind? . . . Little Marty, you always called me. Well, Mom, you always wanted me to grow up to be like your brother. The son-of-a-bitch. Informing on his own son was bad enough. Did he have to bug his room? And take pictures? What a family! But we've been through all that. I still laugh every time I think of that catcher's mitt he sent me with the Dodgers' names all over it and the autograph from Mel Ott saying To A Real Boy and how I sold it to Jumbo. Stupid bastard. And he thought *he* was getting the better part of the deal. Well, anyhow—keep all this under your hat, it's strictly confidential, as they say, but if you can't trust your own mother and father and your Uncle Marty, who *can* you trust? Be good now, and take care, will you? Amy's at the hospital visiting her mother and things don't look too good, I'm afraid. We'll know more after the operation. . . ."

She turns it off. "I told him never to get involved . . . The FBI. And the CIA. What does he need money for? His wife works. It's his father—always putting pressure on him . . ."

She goes to the machine. "He's got to be spoken to."

I get up.

"Where are you going?"

"I thought you'd want to be alone."

"Wait. I want to introduce you."

"Introduce me?"

"To Danny. On tape."

"He doesn't want to meet me."

"Of course he does. You're sleeping in his bed."

She threads the tape and sets up the camera.

"Now say hello and tell him who you are."

The camera starts to hum and I say, "Hello, I'm Nick. Your mother's right here."

"Hello, darling. Meet Nick. He walked into our store and we took him home with us."

She's still behind the camera while I stand there.

"Isn't he handsome? You should see him work. Your father can finally slow down, maybe even take me on a vacation. How would you like visitors? Don't get scared. We'll stay at a motel. Nick'll watch the store for us, as soon as he's broken in."

I smile like an idiot, control an urge to bark.

"Say good-bye now," she whispers.

"So long," I wave.

She comes alongside me and gives me a hug.

"My Number-Two Son," she tells him. "Now listen to *me*, Number One. . . ."

I inch out of the picture and leave the room.

"Just 'cause you were on television doesn't mean you know more than your mother. What's this business with the CIA?" As I close the door: "You've got a wife and son now. And a sick father . . ."

Later, before bed, she kisses me good night. "I'm so glad you're here. Do you think he'll make it? If he can just hold out . . . He's got what it takes . . ."

"He'll make it," I assure her.

6

I should have left. Don't ask me why I didn't. I kept telling myself—the shad, soon as I get inside one, I'll be on my way. In the meantime, there was the sixty a week clear, no take-out, under-the-table, they called it. And all the free fish I could eat. Besides, what was the rush? There's this kid I met on the subway once who wanted to know if we were on the Express. When I asked him what stop he wanted, he shrugged and said: "I just gotta keep moving." I understood that kid, I should've remembered him. At the time, though, I thought: Where was I running? Canada? Mexico? My luck, I'd have run right into another fish store.

Not that I believe I'm a victim of fate or any of that bullshit. I still think Oedipus could have *ig-*

nored that oracle and stayed where he was—but that would have *really* taken guts. The same goes for Joseph K. Sure Kafka's saying you can't beat the System, but look at that great scene in the Cathedral when the Priest calls K by name and K stands there for a minute realizing he doesn't *have* to answer or turn around, he can just keep going.

Danny was the other reason I stayed. I actually liked the sweaty bastard. Turning him on every night, my own private situation comedy, soap opera, Mighty Mouse serial. He reminded me of this professor I had who supported our demands for a student strike. When I didn't consult or confide in him one week, he got vicious and attacked: "Do you realize I alienated my colleagues, risked my tenure for *you*?" I told him I thought he did it for himself —for what he believed in. And what the hell did he think the strike was? Some goddam teacher popularity contest? He had the same look, the same hunger in his eyes as Danny. Cut open anything he did—no matter how honorable—and there was this eight-year-old kid inside who just wanted to stand out and be recognized.

The point is, I stayed. Mighty Mouse, the shad, Mr. and Mrs. Joe, the sixty a week, the free fish, free rent, the warm bed, whatever. If Fate and I had an appointment, I'd find out what it was for. *Then* I'd break it or keep it.

My hope was I wouldn't show up.

In the meantime, I wore my galoshes and *watched*. And by the time we were into March I was boning porgies, flounders, shucking clams. Joe never let on he was pleased, naturally, but at least he was letting me do it without standing over my shoulder anymore. He was even going out for coffee.

Then—around the third week it was—everything started to go off at once, like a pinball machine.

First, the landlord, then the real estate lawyer. To make a long story short, Joe's Fish Market became an oil well. Nobody could mention names yet, but according to the kosher butcher this lawyer's client—the jeweler two doors down heard it was a bank—wanted to buy up the whole block, and who had the choicest property, who was the last merchant on the street to even dream of giving up such a booming business no matter what they offered him for his lease—you guessed it.

The fighting must have gone on for a month. Not that the client was definite, he was just expressing interest, just "shopping," the lawyer said, but as far as *Mrs.* Joe was concerned, the deal was all sewed up. The hot dog lady and her ninety-six-year-old mother had held out for a quarter of a million five years ago when they came around the corner to put up that fancy apartment building with the sauna and tennis court on top of it, and before that you couldn't even *give* that store away.

"What would you do with all that money?" Joe

asked her. "Sit on your ass all day around a swimming pool?"

"I'll worry about that when they make out the check."

He still held out. Not because he was shrewd or a gambler by nature. He really wasn't sure he wanted to sell.

Then the lawyer finally *did* come up with an offer—$150,000—and Mrs. Joe almost collapsed.

"I'd never have to touch a fish again," she said. "I could be a woman for the first time in my life."

"What have you been until now?" he asked.

"A thing," she told him. "A *smelly* thing."

He still held out.

"If you're not going to think of *me*, think of your health," she tried.

"I'd rather die in my boots than over a crap table in Vegas."

"You could finally have your own studio, *paint* all day. . . ." That got him. He *thought* about it.

"Danny would never have to worry. Like *we* did. The baby would be taken care of for the rest of his life."

She should have quit when she was ahead.

"Let him worry. It's good for him," Joe told her. "The baby'll go to work. Like *I* did."

In desperation, she called Danny, pleaded with him to persuade his father.

"This is costing me money," Joe said, on the extension. "If I sell, I'll send you a check so I can call you collect."

She finally gave up, withdrew. "*You* talk to him. He'll listen to you."

"I'm only a stranger," I said.

"But he likes you. He has respect. Talk to him, we'll take good care of you."

I talked to him. The lawyer said he'd give him one more week to make up his mind. If he didn't sell, the whole deal would fall through, every merchant on the block would have his ass.

"You could open up another place," I told him. "Fish and chips, like you've been talking about. Your customers can eat them the way they do in England —out of newspaper."

"And who'd cook? You? You think she'd ever step foot in another fish place?"

"I'll be around. We'll get help."

He called the lawyer. "*Two* hundred thousand or no deal."

The lawyer didn't return the call.

She panicked. "Call him again. Tell him you'll take a hundred seventy-five."

The kosher butcher came in and started screaming. "You trying to kill me? You got something against me? What did I ever do to you?"

He called.

One hundred fifty. That was it.

"I'll take it."

Mrs. Joe let out a yell. And kissed me hard on the mouth.

"You brought us luck," she says later, buying me a suit. "We're going out to celebrate."

"Not *me*," Joe says. "I don't go anywhere till there's a signature."

"Then we'll go *without* you," she says. And gets tickets to a Wednesday matinee.

"What's the matter? You can't go on a Saturday?" Joe says.

"I want Nick to have a day off. Besides, the seats are cheaper. And I don't like leaving you alone in the house. This way I know you're in the store."

Wednesday morning, when she thinks I'm still downstairs picking up some groceries and cigars for her, the bathroom door is open and I catch a glimpse of her in the stall shower—blurred and wavy with big red nipples. Then just before she takes me out to lunch, another tape arrives.

"We'll watch later," she says. "You gotta get to Charleston Garden early."

Even early, we wait on line in this ladies' tearoom done up like a plantation on the eighth floor of B. Altman's department store. Aside from me, the only other person there with testicles is a twelve-year-old bisexual cleverly disguised as a midget gigolo lighting mommy's cigarette while she gives me the eye. Everybody else is either a nun or a sweet old lady with bald spots. Mrs. Joe eats it up. The blueberry muffins, the weeping willow wallpaper, the white columns, the veranda. She orders a Spring Forecast which promises tomato wedges, cucumber slices, carrot curls, and cottage cheese on garden greens. I order a hamburger but they've never heard of it. So I settle for a Peter Pail Picnic Lunch which gives me my own pail and shovel, a cream cheese and jelly sandwich, a brownie, a lollipop, milk, and a prize which turns out to be a green and rubber troll.

"You're crazy," she laughs.

I put the troll on my finger and wave all its arms and legs.

"If only Joe could learn to relax. What good is money if you don't know how to enjoy yourself?"

"Give him time. He's gotta get used to it."

"How much time does he have?" She gives me a look I don't quite understand. "He's not as strong as he makes out. He puts on a big front—for *you.*"

"For me?"

"You don't sleep with him. You don't hear the way he breathes at night. Or see him take his insulin."

"I still can't keep up with him when we go to the market."

"Fish is his adrenalin. He can't live without it."

I tell her about our idea for a fish and chips place.

"Are you crazy? He'll have me there day and night."

"He's already agreed. Just me and hired help."

"You? What do you want to tie yourself down for? You're young. And healthy. It's time you went back to school."

"Not yet."

She gives me one of her looks. "I don't understand you. If you were my son, I'd be worried sick."

I smile and pat her hand.

She clutches it. "Come *with* me."

I look around. "Where?"

"Wherever we go. Wherever we end up. What am I going to do with all that money? With *him*? I need you. To help me spend it."

I open my mouth and laugh. All the bald spots look up.

She tightens, like a fist, and calls the waitress.

"I'm sorry," I tell her.

"We're late. It's a two o'clock curtain."

Then getting up and opening her bag: "Here." She slips me a ten. "I don't think a woman should pay."

The show's at another Garden, *Winter* this time, same as Charleston—lots of ladies, mommies' gigolos all grown up. We sit in the first-row mezzanine flanked by troops from Great Neck—the uniform mink with orange hair.

"These weren't easy to get," she says. "It's the latest hit. I still don't know why Danny doesn't write one of these things. He could make a fortune."

One of these things is a dinosaur—a musical monster with a hundred movable parts—arms, legs, asses, sets—all controlled by the same switch—oiled, synchronized, precisely coordinated—a perfect shell—like at the Museum of Natural History—with no insides.

The scary thing is it wants you to laugh and cry, react to it as human, funny, real. Every song it sings taps a Universal Emotion sure it can count on us for the appropriate response. Songs of Love and Loneliness and Ambition and Time and Friendship and Freedom and Defeat and Survival sung Happily, Sadly, Cynically, Fiercely—to appropriate rhythms with appropriate faces—in ventriloquist voices hidden in mikes booming like echoes out of canyon throats.

To make things worse, the audience loves it. The Minks gush, the Boys fall all over themselves. This one was a movie—a Late Show regular—the plot's been updated and the star's from Hollywood, big in the forties and famous for her legs. She kicks one in the air and they all have heart attacks. Then, the number they've all been waiting for: Legs, alone, her man's walked out, nothing but a spotlight, she lets them have it. Before the curtain's down, they're up as one, Minks and Boys cheering their dream: Woman With Balls. Who needs men? Men are Losers, Chumps, Brutes. Fuck 'em. Do without 'em. Fuck your Self.

Intermission, she points out a fag: "Isn't he cute? Look at those pants. You can see his *business* from over here." He catches her eye and gives her a smile. She blushes and laughs and looks away.

"You've got a friend." I tell her.

"Just my type."

She pretends to be insulted, sneaks another look. I feel like an intruder at a secret wedding.

Act Two. More of the same. Legs Beats Rival, Age. Men. But she learns to be humble and say please and to cut off just enough so he won't miss it.

The audience leaves thinking art is machinery, Late Show intact, warmed-over, reaffirmed: We're Only Human. Compromise Is Maturity. Pain Always Pays Off. Money Isn't Everything. "But did you see those costumes? You could feed starving children for a year with what they cost. And did you read about the composer? Forty-five thousand a week. His father died, his mother gave piano lessons. . . ."

Back home, she mixes Manhattans. "I hate the taste, but I love the cherry. Put the tape on, will you? I'll call the store."

She asks Joe how he is, if he's survived without her. "Good," she says, " 'cause I'm not coming back. And bring home Chinese food. I'm not cooking, either." She hangs up and comes inside.

"To the future," she says, and takes a sip. Then

the wince and the giggle: "I'm drunk already." She fakes a stagger and swoons to the sofa. "It's about time my *hero* woke up. He hasn't said hello for over a month."

I turn on the tape, take my seat beside her, we both drink, and she leans against me.

Amy sits before us under a humming bonnet, nursing the baby, drying her hair.

"There are some things you can do nothing about." Danny's voice, but Amy doesn't seem to hear him. "My wife, for example. You wouldn't believe it to look at her, but she's got this smell. Nothing serious. Under her breath. Like asparagus. I hate asparagus. It makes me sick." Amy looks up, squints to read his lips.

"Sometimes when the wind is right it goes away. But then it comes back stronger than before."

She shrugs and shakes her head and points to the bonnet.

"I look at other people to see if *they* smell it. But they're too polite or they like asparagus."

She says, "I can't hear you."

He comes into the picture and kisses her on the mouth. A plane flies over and she holds her ear.

"I said you smell."

"What?" Amy says.

"What *is* this? What kind of joke?" Mrs. Joe puts her drink down, demands an answer.

Amy shrugs hopelessly. Danny looks at us and smiles. Then he comes forward and blacks himself out.

Mrs. Joe looks at me, confused, frightened. The scene changes to Danny in a chair, sitting there with a vacuum cleaner, caved in, out of breath.

"I can't stop. I go on these binges. Yesterday, ironing. Today, vacuuming. I walk around the room setting clocks, polishing surfaces, arranging knickknacks. Last week I did nothing but shop. Make out lists in alphabetical order. God forbid I should get caught short—without soap, toilet paper, instant pizza. I can't go out without picking up matchsticks. Butts. Gum wrappers. Off lawns, driveways, the floors of stores. Look at that crumb. Just *sitting* there . . ."

He closes his eyes and clenches his fists.

"Dear God, let me leave it. Let it breed flies. . . ." Rising ferociously, he switches on the vacuum, coming toward us, attacking the crumb.

The phone rings. Another blackout. It rings again and we realize it's ours. But then another scene and neither of us moves.

Danny, in pajamas, sitting in the dark: "Two weeks after the operation and she can't walk without terrible effort . . ."

The phone stops.

"Yet even when I remember it's the nurse's day off, I don't hang up. I let it ring. And watch her in my mind as she struggles out of bed, inches down the hallway, stopping, swallowing, holding on to the walls, picking up the phone, gasping for breath . . . Hello, Ma. Are you all right? I thought the nurse was there. I'm terribly sorry. I just wanted you to know I'd be a little late. Go back to bed. I shouldn't have disturbed you. . . ."

He sits there a minute, then gets up. Next, the baby, crawling in his playpen, Janis Joplin screaming, then Danny in his shorts, gyrating, humping, driven, sweaty, dancing around the baby, like some savage rite.

Mrs. Joe stands up. The picture changes. Somebody, a stranger, then I realize it's Danny, sitting in the chair, with a full head of hair.

"Oh my God." She sits. "He's wearing a wig."

Danny stares at us, then suddenly erupts, giggling, laughing, doubling over.

Next, just eyes. Then he sits back. Long look, like into a mirror, until he spits, splattering the lens.

Mrs. Joe gasps, squeezing my hand, bending my fingers till my nails cut my palms.

Danny, in a robe now, smiling strangely. He lets the robe drop and stands there naked.

The phone rings and we both jump. It rings again and I go toward Danny as he walks toward me into a close-up of his penis.

I turn off the machine and answer the phone.
"Hello."

"Who's this?"

"Nick. Who's this?"

"Oh," he says. "This is Danny. How come you're home? Not in the store?"

"It's my day off."

"My father's getting generous. Where's my mother?"

"She's right here. But she's not feeling too well."

"What's the matter? Can't I speak to her?"

"She's lying down. I'll see if she's up."

I go inside, she's exactly how I left her, sitting there dazed, her eyes wild with thought.

"It's Danny," I tell her.

She looks at me, frozen.

"I told him you were sick. But you'd better speak to him."

A long minute, then she gets up. I run to catch her, help her to the phone.

"Danny?"

"Mom?" He's practically shouting. I stand there supporting her, listening in. "What's the matter? I tried you five minutes ago. I called the store, no answer there either. Are you all right? What's wrong?"

"A little virus."

"You sound terrible."

"I took a pill. It knocked me out."

"Where's Dad? Why didn't he answer?"

"You must have missed him. He's on the way home."

"Well, look, I'm calling 'cause I did something stupid. I sent you a tape of something I'm working on instead of the one you were supposed to get."

"Working on?"

"Something crazy. If you ever saw it, you'd think I was nuts. Did you get it yet? I sent it out Monday."

She looks at me. "I got it."

"You didn't play it, did you?"

"It just came."

"Well, *don't*, will you? Send it back. You'd never understand it and it would only upset you."

"Why? What's in it?"

"The other tape will explain everything. Remember a sweetheart named Harry Nichols? Well, guess who called at six in the morning. Almost two years I haven't heard from the bastard. *Now* he wakes up, wants to do things for me. His picture grossed over fourteen million. If I could just send him something, an idea, a couple of pages, so he can show it around, bring me out there to write it. So I sent him something. I still haven't heard from him, but that's what this crazy tape's about. This character who turns informer, sends a Mexican kid to the electric chair for sabotaging a war game, wiping out a town. I'm using the machine to get to know him, act out his life, you know—improvise . . ."

"I know." She sounds better.

"So just send it back, okay, old buddy? The other tape is on the way."

"Wait. How's the baby?"

"What baby? He's taller than I am."

She laughs and nods at me as if to say everything's all right now.

"And tell my father he's got it backwards. It's the *help* that works, the *boss* who takes the day off."

"You know your father." She shrugs at me.

"Well, he doesn't have to sell now, either. Let him stay put, if he wants to. You'll come out and stay with us. In California."

"Don't tempt me. And don't be such a big shot, either. You're not in Hollywood yet."

"That reminds me. I didn't make this collect."

"You didn't? What kind of a stupid thing was that to do?"

"Good-bye, old buddy."

"What's your father going to do with all his money?"

Click.

She hangs up. "I knew there was an explanation." I smile.

"I'm only sorry *you* had to see it."

"I won't say anything."

"That's not what I meant. I wouldn't want it to upset you."

"I'm not upset."

"Can you imagine the nerve of that Nichols? After two years—six in the morning?"

She goes inside and rewinds the tape. "I still don't understand why he had to use Amy and the baby and his mother-in-law like that."

"That's what all writers do."

"What?"

"Use a little of themselves to get their imaginations going."

"That's his trouble. Too much imagination. Ever since he was a kid, I never knew *when* he was telling me the truth." She puts the tape back in the box. "Why can't he write something down-to-earth, like that show we saw this afternoon?"

"This looks more interesting."

She laughs. The phone rings.

"Who's that now?"

She goes back inside. "My luck, it'll be Joe—telling me the store burned down. Or the lawyer saying the deal is off, his client went bankrupt, or dropped dead . . . Hello? . . . Yes? . . . Who's this? . . . The *Police?*" I go inside.

"An accident? What kind of accident?"

She reaches out for me. "Beat up?"

I stand behind her and we listen together: "Just before closing . . . a couple of addicts, we think . . . hit him over the head with a gun and emptied the register . . ."

"Oh my God . . . Joe . . ."

I take the phone. "Is he alive? Is he okay?"

"He's in Emergency. At Lenox Hill . . ."

"He's dead. I know it."

"He's okay," I tell her. And take down the address.

7

We felt like accomplices. If we hadn't gone to the matinee and left him alone, it never would have happened. He looked terrible. The gun got him in the nose and over the forehead so there were stitches and a big bandage and his eyes were swollen the same color my ears turned when I got drunk the first time—around fifteen—and the friend I was with sobered me up so hard he beat me purple.

The next night when he can sit up, he tells us: "One of them, a real fiend, he looked like, hit me *twice*, and I had already handed over the money."

"Some people just like to beat people up."

"He'd have probably shot me if the phone didn't ring and scare them away."

"That was Danny," she says. "He saved your life."

The doctor comes in and takes his pulse. "Your husband's a lucky man. With his diabetes and heart, though, we have to watch him very carefully. At least a week in the hospital. No store for a month."

Joe explodes. "What are you trying to do? Give me a stroke? Who'll do my buying? Bone my shad?"

"We'll manage," she says. "Like we did today. If we need help, I'll call the Union. In the meantime, be grateful. You've got a boy."

I feel like Pinocchio at Gepetto's deathbed. He winces in pain, says okay, okay, lies back, drugged, and closes his eyes.

"Tomorrow's Friday," she says at home. "Can you handle the market or should I have them deliver?"

"I'll do the buying. I know the order by heart."

"But will you know what's good?"

"I'll use my nose."

Later, after we watch the news and I'm in bed, she comes in to say good night.

"You think I should call Danny? I hate to worry him."

"Whatever you decide."

"I'll wait till next week. When Joe comes home."

She starts to go, then stops in the doorway. Her robe's slightly open, I can see the swoop of her breast. "Except for the week Danny was born, this is the only time in thirty-two years Joe and me have been separated. Before Joe, I shared a room with my sister. My father kept bringing over his relatives from the other side, though, so most of the time we shared the same bed, too. My whole life, I've never slept alone."

She laughs. "I'll set my alarm. And make you breakfast."

She doesn't have to. I'm up at four. Out of the house before she wakes up. I leave a note by her bed: Bring donuts. Speed down the Drive without a license. Race through the market ahead of an imaginary Joe, ordering, sniffing, bargaining, shouting.

"Joe's in the hospital. He'll be back next week."

The caged bookkeeper calls me inside. "I hear he's dying."

"Just a slight concussion."

"Is it true he's going to sell? For a half a million?"

"The papers aren't signed yet. We're still waiting."

"*You're* in on this?" He gives me a smile. "Smart boy." He goes back to his books.

When I get to the store, she's there waiting. I unload, ice, arrange the window and showcase, while she puts up orders, delivers them to the bars, brings back the coffee, and boils the shrimp. We work in silence—me at Joe's board. Like a quarterback and fullback, talking in signals, I hand off the fish, she runs with it and wraps it. Coachless, free, we call our own plays like we've planned it, rehearsed it—in the same dream. She watches me do what Joe hasn't let me—crack open oysters, take his customers—turning every challenge into a performance, a conquest—smiling, winking, leading me on.

Finally, when there's a lull, she sees me looking at a shad.

"We *need* one boned," she says. "People have been asking."

I pick it up and lay it on the board. "I've never done it."

"There's always a first time."

The beginning is easy. Like any other. But then comes the belly, slitting it open, not too deep, mustn't rip the roe. I tear the skin and my hand slips. The incision is crooked, I start again. This time it's straight and I reach in, loosening the membrane, scooping the roe out.

She smiles applause. "We'll put your name on that one." I turn it over into her hand. She lays it on paper in the window, props it up with ice.

I split the fish and remove the backbone, then stand there staring, holding Joe's knife. It looks easy; I go in under. The bones don't lift out, though, so I pull and tweeze them, yanking chunks of meat out like handfuls of hair.

She stands there and winces. I break out in a sweat. My fingers are slimy, I lose my grip. I wipe my hands, attack again, the shad in shreds now, bones intact.

"It's no use. We'll never sell it. You'll try again—when Joe comes back."

I feel sick. The fish looks sicker. I throw it away and scrub my board.

She calls Joe and tells him all about it. They have a good laugh and she smacks him a kiss.

"We'll be there early tomorrow. Get a good night's sleep."

She hangs up. "He sounds better. Our luck, he'll be back Monday."

Two more hours, a hundred more customers. We sell out. Drive home, exhausted.

The tape meant for *her* is there in the mailbox.

"I oughta screen it first," she says. "Like the Catholic Church."

She prepares dinner while I take my bath. I do the dishes while she takes hers. Then meeting in the room like old conspirators, I serve her her ice cream and cigar and turn on her son.

He stands there squinting, talking through buck teeth, with a little mustache, in a Charley Chan accent.

"Herro, you rucky people. This is Number One Son. Well, Number Two, how do you rike it? Mama Chan make you good flied chicken? Number One Father fleeze your ass off?"

He peels off the mustache and puts back his face.

"You really fell in, pal. What a family! Sure you don't want to change your mind? All my life I wanted a brother. All I had to do was leave home. Hi, Mom. Hi, Dad. Am I still in the will? Can I keep the name? No kidding, Nick. Welcome to the clan. If you survive us, you can survive anything. Speaking of survival, you better sit down. When I tell you who called, you'll go into shock . . ."

He tells us about Nichols wanting his ideas.

"I told him one on tape. Wait till you hear it. It's called *Public Spectacle*—about this funny little comic —from Brooklyn originally—whose partner leaves him stranded in this southern Army town. Sound familiar? Not that it's autobiographical, I'm just using the situation. Anyhow, there's this war game going on called Operation Control which they keep playing on local television between old Burt Lancaster movies and Josephine the Plumber commercials. That's the way the picture opens. With this empty electric chair. No titles, and a hooded man is led in. The guards strap him down and the switch is pulled. We watch his body convulse, smoke rise from his head. As a voice tells us: What you have just witnessed is a mock electrocution of a mock student anarchist convicted of sabotage. Just another dramatic illustration of Operation Control's Deterrent System—to reassure the population that in the event of *real* crisis there is no problem that cannot be effectively wiped out. Cut to Josephine—scalding the stains out of her sink. Then cut to an old Mexican in his shack watching the whole thing on TV. Cut to commotion outside—shack on fire—young

Mexican woman screaming, trying to get past soldiers. . . ."

He acts out the parts.

"Sorry, ma'am. We're under orders. This road has become a supply route between the enemy and the guerrillas. We have no choice but to destroy everything on it . . . My house, she screams. My father's in there . . . Sorry, ma'am. We made a thorough search. . . . He's an old man. He hides. He's afraid of strangers. . . . You'll have everything you need, ma'am. In the next hamlet. Just get on the truck with everyone else. . . . Cut to interior, the old Mexican in front of the TV watching his own shack burn, his daughter being carried off to the truck, screaming Papa . . . Papa, the old man senile, laughing, as we cut to his shack—outside again—going up in flames, and pull back over a small crowd watching Burt Lancaster, the Rams, the burning shack, *itself*—on multiple screens in the window of the town television store. Get the picture? Get the idea? Mock war starts getting real and everybody thinks it's the Ed Sullivan Show. Until every day, there's another accident, each one worse, more mysterious than the day before, until finally there's this *real* disaster—I haven't figured out what yet—something that practically wipes out the entire town—like an escape of toxic gas, maybe—the point is, *somebody* must be responsible for this deadly sabotage—and that's where our comic comes in. Who runs an Employment Agency for the FBI servicing oversexed security risks with sexy Mexican caddies and baby-sitters? You betcha. Our kid from Brooklyn. Poor bastard. He didn't know what he was getting into. Cause it's up to *him*, see? When the FBI arrests this Chicano kid, it's Brooklyn they count on to supply the evidence. If he doesn't cooperate, they'll arrest *him*—for pimping and prostitution. But you're the Boss, he tells them. You put me in business. Not us, says the FBI. You must have us mixed up with the CIA. Besides, it's your patriotic duty. Without a saboteur, how will the country get a good night's sleep again?

"Well, it just so happens, Brooklyn isn't too fond of Chicano—they've both been screwing the same nymphomaniac wife of the same homosexual Air Force Officer—and Brooklyn's got this thing on Chicano providing her with better service—which Nympho is only too happy to assure him is true. So when Chicano refuses to tell Brooklyn whether he's innocent or not—'The FBI says I'm guilty, let them prove it,' says Chicano—Brooklyn becomes convinced Chicano *is* guilty and comes up with what the FBI's been asking for.

"I'm not sure what the evidence will be yet—something of Nympho's obviously—to establish her as the source of secret information—but it'll be something simple—like it always is—a typewriter, a radio

—just enough to nail Chicano and send him to the chair.

"So. Mock war becomes real. So does mock electrocution. And just in case you haven't guessed yet —we get to watch it on television. Network, this time. Just another dramatic illustration of how far Control can go.

"Are you ready? Here comes the finish. Empty electric chair. Just like the fade-in. Only this time there's a phone next to it so Chicano can call the President and say I'm sorry right up to the last minute. In other words, it's not too late. All he has to do is confess and name his accomplices and he can get clemency, spare his parents. Who are *there,* by the way, to pull the switch. . . .

"'We no Communisto, we Americano,' says Mama, warming up her hands. And where's Brooklyn? A big hero now. Booked into all the big resorts —in Vegas, the Catskills, Miami Beach—as That Great American, that Super-Patriot, the Spy Who Came In From Canarsie—and who's here tonight to make you laugh—the one, the only—doing his act —in front of a huge TV showing the empty electric chair—while the audience waits for Chicano to be led in.

"And does Chicano talk? Does he spare his folks? Does he reach for that phone and make a person-to-President? No, Sir. The switch is pulled. But not before Brooklyn competes and makes a public spectacle of himself. 'Talk. Tell them,' he yells at the screen. '*I'm* your accomplice. It was *my* idea. It's *me* who should be punished. *Me* forgiven.'

"The body convulses and the smoke rises. Hold and fade-out as the voice tells us: What you have just witnessed is a *real* electrocution of a *real* anarchist convicted of sabotage. The first of a series brought to you as a Public Service to assure the population—in light of the mysterious smell reported to be spreading through different parts of the country—that there is no problem, no crisis, that cannot, *will* not, be effectively wiped out. . . .

"Well? What do you think? Will the movie moguls pay a million in advance for it? What I really want to do is get into Brooklyn's character—his panic, his relationships—show all the things in a person's life he *can't* control or wipe out, like fears and fantasies, dying, hate. Working your balls off and never making it, balding, body odor, memories, guilt. Not loving the people you're supposed to— your wife, your kid, your parents, yourself . . . While the television keeps insisting everything is solvable, all you need is Josephine, an electric chair. Which only makes us more hysterical, heightens the urgency to buy the product. The product in *this* case is Operation Control, a gargantuan mirror of Brooklyn's madness—private hysteria turned into public spectacle. The idea being that we *need* crisis, even *create* it, so we can have the stage to act out our fantasies, blow things up till they're no longer real. Only then, when it's all a performance, do we dare, as actors, to do what we fear: Kill the self that scares us—in the form of Chicanos—with God on our side and without getting punished. The only hitch is, we *need* punishment. The eye in our soul never shuts. Punishment and redemption are what Brooklyn's looking for, what he buys vicariously when they pull that switch. Instant retribution for all his crimes—wishes and betrayals and domestic 'murders'—all those crimes for which there *are* no punishment—which we get away *with,* but never *from.*"

He stops, exhausted, takes a deep breath.

"So what else is new? See any good movies lately? I'll let you know when I leave for Hollywood. In the meantime—I've got a heavy date."

He does his Groucho.

"With a nympho CIA agent who can't get enough of me."

He turns himself off.

She looks at me. "They're going to pay him for that? I didn't understand one word."

"I did."

"You and him. You'll be the only ones in the movie theater. What does he mean *not loving the people you're supposed to?* I never heard such nonsense."

She gets up, wraps her robe around her.

"Electric chairs. Phones. Switches. Televisions.

What is he? A writer or a repair man? If I wasn't there at his delivery, I wouldn't believe he was mine."

She clears away the ashtray, the ice-cream dishes.

"His father. That's who he belongs to. My two artists."

She goes into the kitchen and comes back.

"Sick in the head. *Both* of them."

I laugh. She frowns. Then she smiles, in spite of herself.

"I can't see straight."

"You worked hard today."

She stands there, groggy, closes her eyes. "Tomorrow the hospital." She makes a face. Tired, but relaxed, she looks younger. I catch her in a yawn with a kiss on the cheek.

Startled, she coughs, opens her eyes.

"Get some sleep."

She looks like a kid. Surprised. Pleased. Respectful. Obedient.

"You, too," she whispers. And goes to bed.

Joe feels better, sits up like a king, impatient and fussy when it's only us, a real musketeer with his nurses and visitors.

Brothers and sisters arrive all morning, each one Joe in a different disguise: short, plump, white-haired, bald, behind glasses, mustaches, enormous bosoms. All of them stiff-necked and straight-backed with scallop skin and pot bellies which shake when they laugh while the rest of them sits there. Joe thrives, doing his routine, acting out the theft in a running monologue, as Mrs. Joe rolls her eyes, yawns, makes faces behind their backs.

We go out to lunch and she boils over: "All they do is laugh and cater to their brother. Especially now that he's selling the store. He's the only one who ever made a penny. If it wasn't for me, he'd be just like they are."

We get back and come in on a fight. Joe's sister Irene, huffing and puffing. "It's not right. They shouldn't be there alone."

"Who?" says Mrs. Joe.

They look up, caught.

Joe laughs. "You and Nick. My sister's worried about your reputation."

"At *my* age, I want the neighbors to talk."

"Someone should sleep there," Irene says.

"You volunteering? Whose bed? Mine or Nick's?"

Everybody laughs. The bellies shake.

"Tell them about yesterday," Joe says. "What the shad looked like when he got through with it."

"Butchered, naturally. What did *you* do the first time?"

Joe laughs and makes an announcement: "He pulled out the meat and left the bones."

Bellies shake. I stand there grinning.

Outside the hospital, we all say good-bye. As soon as they leave: "How do you like that bitch? *She's* worried about *my* reputation. It would serve them right. Putting the idea in our heads."

Home, we watch television without our shoes, nibbling Chinese spare ribs and sucking our fingers.

The Million Dollar Movie is *Double Indemnity*—about a blonde who gets an insurance agent to kill her husband. They almost get away with it, but then they shoot each other. The whole thing's in flashback told by the insurance agent while he sits there bleeding into a tape recorder.

"I love Barbara Stanwyck."

"She looks like she's in drag."

"What's drag?" she asks.

"Dressed up like a woman."

She looks at me, confused.

"When you're *really* a man."

"Oh," she says, and turns up her nose. Drag or not, Barbara gets through to me, then, watching the news, we're in for a surprise.

"Organization Cleansweep," the commentator tells us, "a peacetime war exercise in its sixth month now seems to be turning into the real thing. For a look at *that* story, we take you to Chris Baker, San Lorenzo, Texas . . ."

We look at each other, then at Chris.

"Nobody can really believe what's happening here in this old Army town not far from the Alamo.

Some people are calling it sabotage, others just a run of bad luck. Whatever you call it, today's disaster taking the lives of a dozen children comes on the heels of a whole series of mysterious happenings, and the town's demanding a full-scale investigation."

"It's those hippies from New York," a man in shirt-sleeves yells, grabbing the mike away. "They've infiltrated the Army, the Air Force, the Marines . . ."

"Thank you very much," Chris says, yanking the mike back. "I'm standing in front of San Miguel's Church where only two hours ago a parachute drop of heavy equipment failed to open—trucks, tanks, and tractors—falling free on a busload of children, killing twelve and injuring twenty, as the children ran out to watch and catch them . . ."

A suspended helicopter starts to rise.

"You can see their bodies being lifted away now."

A full and bulky net rises with it.

"Last week, work on a missile project had to be suspended indefinitely due to the invasion of over a million mosquitoes."

A man with his face bandaged talks into the mike. "I don't know where they came from. You coulda put saddles on them."

"And only the day before, a pack of dogs, specially trained to sniff out marijuana, went wild on a rampage, attacking an Indian reservation, a shopping center, and a Texaco gas station. The most serious thing to happen, though, until now, was the stockade knifing in their sleep of a group of soldiers, who, under orders to play homosexuals, were rounded up and put in isolation as part of Organization Cleansweep's campaign against Perversion and Deviation."

He hands the mike over. "What do *you* think, sir?"

"That's Danny," she calls out.

"Is it all a coincidence? Or do you agree it's a conspiracy?"

"I wouldn't know," Danny says. "I'm just here taking pictures."

"Thank you. This is Chris Baker, San Lorenzo, Texas . . ."

"Just like his movie," she says. "I don't believe it."

The phone rings and she runs to get it.

"Danny? Is that you? We just saw you . . . Nick, it's Danny . . . pick up the extension."

I go into the bedroom and listen in.

". . . I waited till eleven thirty *your* time just in case they played it. Isn't that incredible? Talk about life imitating art. I'm afraid to go to sleep . . . dream . . . wake up . . . Just two hours ago, there was a terrible crash. A planeload of replacements into a drive-in movie screen: *2001*. The pilot got confused. Saw these spacemen coming toward him—tried not to hit them. The whole screen went up in flames. Cars trapped, crashing, running people over.

Wait, you'll see, they won't be satisfied, the pilot was a hippie, a student anarchist . . ."

"Are you all right? Is the baby safe?"

"Where's Dad? Didn't he see it?"

"How's Amy? How's her mother?"

"Put Dad on. I'll say hello."

"Your father's not here."

"Where is he?"

She waits for a second. "He's in the hospital."

"Why didn't you tell me?"

"It's nothing to worry about."

"What is it? A stroke?"

"He got beat up. In the store. By junkies."

"Oh my God. When did it happen?"

"This past Wednesday."

"Where were *you*?"

"I went to a show."

"Don't you work anymore? Where was Nick?"

"Nick was with me. To help me celebrate."

"Celebrate what? Dad getting beat up?"

"Selling the store. And lower your voice."

"What the hell's going on there?"

"We're having an affair."

"That's not funny."

"You shouldn't have asked."

Long wait. While we all breathe. Then Danny with a laugh, in his kid voice: "Sorry, old buddy. I got upset. You know I can't stand it when you guys get sick."

"We'll try to live forever so you never have to worry."

"You're really angry."

"I've had enough. If it isn't your father, it's his fucking family. If it isn't them, it's my own son."

"I'll call you tomorrow."

"That's up to you."

She hangs up and I go inside.

"I have a headache," she says. "I'm going to bed."

She walks past me and closes her door.

All day Sunday we repeat Saturday, more bellies, more monologue, more cologne, while she sits at his feet, a silent queen, unsmiling, hidden, behind dark glasses.

"*I* get beat up, *she* gets a migraine. She's jealous," Joe explains. "Wants attention. The day I die, *she'll* commit suicide."

I take her home early to Danny's call, warm up pot roast while she yes's and no's him: "Yes, I understand . . . No, I'm not still angry . . . Lenox Hill, I'm sorry, I thought I told you . . . Yes, call him now . . . No, you won't disturb him . . ."

We sit down to eat and he calls again.

"I told you he was okay . . . it was just a scare . . . What do you want Nick for?" She looks at me and shrugs.

I wipe my mouth. "Hello?"

"Nick?"

"Hi, Danny."

"I just want to thank you for taking care of Mom. Dad tells me you're terrific, that you're even boning shad."

"Not exactly."

"Well, I wish I could be there, but I'm really swamped. Tell Mom I'll call her soon as I hear from Hollywood."

"Good luck."

"I can use it."

We both wait.

"Well, okay . . . No hard feelings, I hope."

"None at all."

"So long, buddy."

I return to the table where we eat without talking. She picks at her food, then gets up.

"I oughta fire you," she says. "For your own good."

I look up. She goes to the stove.

"It would save you the trouble of deciding to leave us."

"I'm not going anywhere."

"Why not?"

She pours my coffee and stands above me.

"You're fired," she says.

"Okay, I'm fired."

We both wait for the other to smile. Instead, her eyes fill and she puts down the coffee, walking regally, furiously, out of the room.

That night I have the dream: Undeveloped negative, transparent, faceless. King and Queen. Me and Danny. The King blesses us, sends us off to War. Cut to battle, Danny fighting off soldiers, someone behind him sneaking up with a knife. I raise mine, but keep it suspended, letting Danny get it before I kill his murderer. The soldiers cheer as I stand there, bloody, and carry me, a hero, back to the King, who kisses and embraces me and crowns me with garlands and makes me his son and gives me his queen.

Next morning at the market, I buy extra shad, keep them hidden at the store under crabs and seaweed. She comes in around nine with danish and coffee, puts up some orders, and signs some checks.

Then around ten thirty, opening the mail, she clutches a letter and says: "We got it."

"Got what?"

"The papers. The sale. They just want our signatures and it's all set."

"Congratulations."

"I gotta see Joe."

She puts on her coat. "I'll be back later."

"Take the day off. I'll meet you at the hospital."

She smiles okay and rushes out.

My original idea was to send her home early; now I have the morning, I take out a shad. The first one, I mutilate, just like the last, the second one, less so, at least I get the bones out. Between customers,

I practice all day, my thumbs and fingers moist like butter, up to the knuckles, probing each fold. The sixth shad I wrap like a gift, close five minutes early, take it with me.

Waiting at the hospital is Joe's signature.

"We're rich," she says and gives me one of her hard ones.

I give Joe the bag which now has a ribbon.

"What's this?" he asks. "More cologne?"

"Smell it," I smile. "It's the latest thing."

He puts his nose to it, then shrugs at her. She shrugs back and he opens it up.

"It looks like a shad."

"It *is* a shad."

"What do you want me to do? Eat it raw?"

"I boned it myself."

"My God, it's perfect." She looks at me and laughs. "How long did it take you?"

"An hour and a half. But first I threw five in the garbage."

"And *you* made fun of him," she says, to Joe.

"I found a bone," Joe tells me.

"I owe you a quarter."

"Take it back to school with you. Show it to your teachers."

"*You're* my teacher," I tell him.

"*I'm* going to Vegas."

"What about our Fish and Chips?"

"You don't need me. Run your own."
"I couldn't do that."
"Sure you could. You're a smart boy."
He picks up the fish and gives it back.
"Come on," she says. "We'll talk about it tomorrow."
"Leave the papers here."
"Why? What's wrong?"
"I want to read them again. Before I go to sleep."
She hesitates, suspicious, then hands them over.
"Don't stay up too long. You need your rest."

"He's trying to kill me," she says after dinner. "He can't stand to see me live, have a good time."
We're sitting in the living room without the lights on. I can't see her face. Just cigar smoke.
"What good is the money if *he* comes with it?"
"He'll be a new man. You'll start again."
"I wish he would die and leave me in peace."
The phone rings and she just sits there. I get up and answer it.
"Nick?"
"Danny?"
"Put Mom on, will you."
I go back inside and tell her who it is. She sighs, exhausted, and takes the call.
I go into my room and close the door, get undressed, and into bed.

She walks in, without knocking.

"He's coming home."

"What happened?"

"They bought the idea. For three thousand dollars. Not enough to live on, so he called his father to borrow five thousand more. When Joe got on, Danny says he sounded funny. If he didn't know him better, he'd say he caught Joe crying. Just dozing, Joe told him. Lying there and thinking. For the first time he talked to Danny about dying, how his life was over, how he didn't care. 'Your mother has money now,' he said. 'What does she need me for? Let her find a young one, live it up.'"

She stops, choked, between pity and disgust.

"'I'm coming home,' Danny told him. 'I can write anywhere. Just so long as I get out of Texas. We'll all be together again, the whole family. Even Amy's mother. Who's dying of cancer.'"

She looks at me, scared, her eyes swollen.

"Joe told him: 'Live where you want, I'll send you *ten* thousand, don't worry about *me*.' 'We'll see,' Danny told him, 'I'll talk to Amy.' He just told me he's made up his mind. 'For the first time,' he said, 'I felt like his son.'"

We look at each other, then she says it.

"One more week and they'll both be here."

My heart beats like it wants to come out. I swallow dry and remove the blanket.

"I'm ignorant," she says. "You'll have to tell me."
Smiling, I reach out. She comes and sits beside me.
"Next April, I'll be fifty."
I place her hand.
"How old is your mother?"
I shrug. She strokes me.
"My mother died when she was fifty-one. I was younger than you are. Seventeen."
Like a cat, I extend, and open her robe.
"My father, they said, would never survive. He buried two more wives and outlived her to eighty."
Exposing her breasts, I harden in her hand.
"My name is Betty. Not Mrs. Joe."
"Betty," I whisper.
Her nails make me shout it.
"My mother loved me. *I* was her life."
Squeezing hold of her breasts, I kiss her open, taste smoke, lick away cobwebs.
"You shame me," she cries, as I reach under, take her in my hand, squirm my fingers. Moist, meaty, she takes them in as I pull on her nipple, lead her down.
"You want what Joe wants. What I never give him."
Up to my knuckles, I fuck her mouth.

TWO

8

Was murder always in my mind? Or only at the moment when it happened?

As it turned out, we had more than a week. Just when Joe was ready to come home, he ran a fever from a sore throat which worried the doctors and kept him there another five days. Danny was delayed until the FBI could replace him.

"God is either being good to us or playing some kind of dirty joke," she laughed.

"There is no God," I said, waiting to be struck dead. "We've killed Him."

Then we'd celebrate by killing Him again.

Even when Joe came home, all he had to do was take a walk or nap. Sometimes, we didn't even wait.

Dinner, her foot would be up against my leg, her hand inside my thigh as she asked him if he wanted more, was there anything else she could give him. The incredible thing is she really did want to make him happy. Not out of guilt or pity, but because she could afford to now. Having attended to her own desire, she could attend to his. When you get right down to it, she was glad to be alive. Having committed a sin and survived, she felt magnanimous, reborn, like a gambler squandering his winnings to show his gratitude, spread his luck.

One night, when Joe was finally up to it and had fallen asleep afterward, she came inside and said, "He's paved the way for you. Make me deeper," which I did, gladly, taking pleasure in what I imagined to be his smell, the danger of his waking up.

"What's gotten into you?" he asked her the next morning. "You'd think I was Cary Grant, the way she waits on me, laughs at all my jokes." What had gotten into her, besides me, was abandon. Even behind his back—when she would squeeze her tits for me—or do things with her tongue—or just sit there, knitting, with her tits out—whenever he dozed while we were watching TV—there was never any malice or mockery in what she did, just daring, recklessness, the simple pleasure of discovering she could do it at all—and not die of judgment or shame.

"I must be a nymphomaniac," she said one Sunday

when Joe went to the store to do his books, coming in to sit on my lap while I sat on the toilet.

"That depends on your definition," I told her.

"Someone who has to have it. All the time."

"Then I must be a nymphomaniac, too," I said, eating her nipples.

"If we could only tell him, *show* him," she said, putting on the tape one Saturday when he went out for a manicure. "So he could see it wasn't so terrible." Instead, we did it for ourselves and erased it and then she cooked him what he liked.

If Danny hadn't come home, we'd have started doing it on the ceiling, out the window. One more month, I told myself. The end of May. When the shad season's over. When Joe doesn't need me anymore.

Need me? What for? To fuck his wife? Okay, when they get the check.

Only the check didn't come. Rumor had it one of the merchants down the street—the shoemaker, they suspected—hearing how much Joe got, decided *he'd* hold out now. It was him and tight money, Joe said. The client, it turned out, was the builder of what was going to be a state-subsidized housing development and he wasn't signing his end of the contract until Albany came through.

"Which could take forever," Betty said. "But who cares as long as *you're* here?"

Which should have been my cue to exit. Only I didn't take it. By the time Danny came home I didn't know whose Oedipus complex I was acting out. His or my own. Did Freud really have it all sewed up? Had I really run away from mine only to run smack into his? Was I really destined, out of vengeance against my mother, to fuck *all* mothers? Turn them *all* into whores? Or did I just like doing it with *this* mother—who wasn't a whore at all, but a mother—who just liked doing it, with me.

And what about Joe? Did I really want to hurt, humiliate him? Is that why I stayed? Hoping he would catch us. Punish us. Or did I hope to please him? The way I thought I was pleasing my father's ghost, by punishing his wife. Was fucking *punishing* her? My cock—a weapon? Like in some lousy novel. Then why did I find pleasure in making her happy? Was I her little boy and she my mommy? Had we pulled The Big One off—free of charge? Or was I just *her* whore—taking her for the money?

What *about* the money? Was I really allergic to it? Or did I have to have it because it was in the family and whatever Joe or Danny had was mine?

How greedy *was* I? Did I really have as much hunger, as much hate in me as Danny? The same need to be Number One. Did my father's hardon really blow my mind? What did I expect him to have there? Do it with? A broomstick? What did

I feel at that moment when he died—going off like a rocket. Loss? Shame? Panic? Disgust? Did I really believe my mother had killed him—or did I only think that afterward when she married his cousin. A dentist. Who did I think I was? Hamlet? If that was the game, whose vengeance was I taking? My father's? Or my own? She had replaced us both. Was *I* her rejected lover? Or was he? Had I become *his* mercenary only to serve *my* revenge? Or was I just daddy's boy—out to win his approval? Would I never stop? Competing? Trying to follow in his cocksteps—until, becoming him and possessing her, I too achieved an orgasmic death?

Bullshit.

I stayed because I was in the middle of a story and I had to finish it.

I stayed to pursue death, not out of any wish or instinct or need to destroy myself, but because death is the end, the logical conclusion of any story, and I had to *know* it—as completely as I could—without dying, thinking I could always get away at the last minute.

I stayed because she kept me hot and made me happy.

I stayed to see how far I would go.

Danny came home the first of June.

This teacher friend of his was going on a year's

sabbatical so he was lucky to get a sublet immediately in a large project on the upper west side.

There was even an extra room for his mother-in-law.

The first time we met was at the party, the big welcome-home at *our* place to celebrate the sales—of the screenplay, the store.

"We don't have the money yet," Joe reminded Betty.

"Then we'll celebrate *again*. When we do."

"Danny doesn't have his money, either," she tells me later. "He got it, but it's all gone—on moving expenses, overdue doctor bills."

"Here," Joe says, just before the guests arrive, reaching into his pocket and throwing something crumpled at Danny across the living room and over the baby in front of me, Betty, Amy, and Frances, her mother. "Writers, like athletes, should be kept hungry. I'll give you the rest when *I* get it."

It doesn't reach. Danny jumps for it. And misses. The baby gets to it first.

Everybody laughs.

"Maybe he should write the movie for me," Danny says.

"Give Daddy the piece of paper, Peter," Amy tells the baby.

Peter puts the check in his mouth.

"Good money? Delicious?" Danny asks.

Peter giggles and chews.

"Spit it out, darling," Betty coaxes. "Here's candy instead."

Peter reaches, but he doesn't get.

"*You* first," Betty tells hm.

Peter looks at his mother, his father.

"Let him eat it," Joe says. "I'll make out another one."

Peter looks at his grandfather.

"That's right," Danny says. "Spit it out—at Grandpa."

Peter hiccoughs and spits it out.

We all applaud.

Peter chuckles and gets the candy.

Danny kneels and picks up the check.

"Thanks, Dad," Amy says.

"That's very generous of you," says her mother. "I wish *I* could help them out."

"We don't need any help, Ma," Danny says. "We just want you to get well . . . Thanks, Dad," he says, flattening out the check, putting it away in his wallet. "I'll pay you back."

He picks up Peter. "Give Grandpa a big kiss."

Peter smacks his chocolate lips.

Everybody aaahs. Danny laughs and leans over to kiss Joe himself.

"What's the matter? *I* didn't work for that money, too?" Betty says.

"I'll get to *you*—later," Danny tells her.

His shirt is full of chocolate. So is Joe's.

"Who's talking to *you*?" Betty answers. "Kiss Grandma," she puckers, her arms out to Peter.

Danny smiles and dumps the baby in her lap.

The bell rings and they cascade in. From Great Neck. Forest Hills. Riverdale. Stamford. Some suntanned up from Florida "now that it's getting hot there," others like bloated corpses fished out of rivers. Joe's family and Betty's and friends from the old days, shrieking and kissing and carrying on. The women—all widows, even those with husbands—garrulous and loud and taut and aggressive—some like Betty with Joes for bosses, some on their own—in real estate, on pensions. Golfers, canasta players, amateur painters, Girl Fridays, grandmothers, skiers, alcoholics. The room is shrill with their raped intelligence as they joke about the money, rub Betty for luck, warn her to spend it—"or the second wife will." While the men—in insurance, zippers, rags, mostly salesmen, manufacturers, one chiropodist, one bookie, one cop, one saloon keeper, somebody whose touch turns everything to gold, another, his brother, whose turns everything to shit—all of them smug, groomed, intact, like specimens of a tribe of fossil boys kept by female keepers who've done their aging for them—pat each other's bellies, tug at crotches, shake Danny's hand for "turning out okay," their own children off in corners—brides, accountants, hippies, interns, somebody who can't make up her mind between a family and show business, son-in-law partners "who fell in good."

I mix their drinks, make conversation. They find out who I am and let Joe have it.

"Hey, Betty. I thought we were friends. If *this* lived in my house, you'd be the first to share it."

"Somebody's gotta put Joe on and take him off."

"Between the two rooms, she must be exhausted."

"I use roller-skates," Betty tells them.

"Hey, Danny, you better grab what you can before your mother gives it away. . . ."

"Hey, Danny. Look who's sleeping in *your* bed . . ." The chiropodist pushes me and Betty together. "What a big mouth you have, Grandma," he says to Betty. "The bigger to eat you with, my dear," he says to me.

"Sssh," his wife says. "The children."

"You've got your fairy tales mixed up, Uncle Ray," Danny tells him.

"As long as I have my *fairies* straight," Ray says, giving me a goose.

Everybody laughs.

"Come to the table, everybody," Betty shouts. "Nick. Help me in the kitchen."

Inside, she gives me a look. And a smile. Danny comes in and gets the message.

"Anything *I* can do?" says Uncle Ray, in a falsetto, coming in behind him and putting his arm around me with his wife's wig on now.

"Why don't you go inside and jerk off?" Danny tells him.

"Danny!" Betty says.

"Sorry, Uncle Ray. I just thought it would put you out of your misery."

Ray's face looks as if it's going to crumble.

"That wasn't nice, Danny," Ray says, and goes out.

"Vultures," Danny says. "Where's my other favorite?"

"I'm warning you," Betty tells him. "I didn't throw a party so you could pick on everybody."

"I just asked where he was."

"My brother Marty will be here," she says. "He had to be in Washington this morning."

"He's already informed on his son Bernie. Who does that leave? His German Shepherd?"

"I want you and Marty to get along this evening," she says firmly. "He's the only brother I have left."

He smiles and takes a swig of his drink.

"Let's you and I get stoned *together* later, okay?" he says to me.

"First you'll eat," Betty says, and starts the parade —of soft-shells on skewers, steamers, shrimp salad, shrimp in sour cream and cognac with marinated mushrooms, lobsters stuffed with almonds, bay scallops in wine, cold salmon—poached—with green mayonnaise, smoked salmon—hot—in custard pie.

They all huddle over the steaming pots, inhaling, eyes closed, in a tribal trance. "Who needs sex? . . .

Who needs money? . . . If I could die right now, I would die happy . . ." They pile it on, take the first taste, stop to swoon, take pity on tongues, speech gives way to slurps, sucks, moans, grunts, ecstasy, orgasm, spiced prayers on oiled and buttered lips, as chins dribble, bodies rock, and everybody licks before he wipes and starts again.

Around the fourth helping, Marty arrives, Danny in his fifties, a Cagney gangster, packed tight and expensive, with a plain, thin wife. The girl with them is lanky and beautiful, with honey hair and shopper's eyes that find Danny, browse through me, as her husband . . . "Marty's eldest . . . his father's right hand" heads for the bar and pours them all doubles.

The big fuss is over Marty's father-in-law—"Elephant Pockets," Danny mutters—a shrunken old man no less than ninety with a face like a walnut and a bulging hernia. Marty helps him to a deep chair where the crowd gathers to kneel at his balls.

"How are you, Ned? . . . You look like a million . . . Getting younger every day . . . Twice as handsome . . ."

The old man grunts and sticks out a pinky.

"Pull that," he commands a nephew.

"Go on. Pull it," an aunt encourages.

The nephew pulls and Ned farts.

"Ever hear one like *that* before? Bottle the smell, you'll make a fortune."

Betty rushes in with introductions. She picks up Peter and shoves him at Marty. "Say hello to your uncle. He's richer than I am."

"Looks just like his father. Poor kid."

Peter spits up on Marty's shoes.

"Bad boy!" Betty says.

"Here. Let *me*." Amy takes him.

"They're all the same," Marty says. His "right hand" wipes his feet. "I got a granddaughter home —just his type."

"Bernie's little girl?"

"We got custody."

"What happened to the mother?"

"We proved her unfit. I didn't set up Howard here in practice for nothing."

Right hand smiles.

"Unfit for what? To be your daughter-in-law?" Danny says. "Or to live in Westchester?"

"We had documented evidence she was addicted to drugs."

"What did you do?" Danny says. "Plant speed in the Pampers?"

"There's food," Betty says. "My shrimp salad."

A cousin comes over and squeezes Marty's arm. "We saw your picture in the paper. It gave us a thrill to cut it out."

"I give you credit," says an uncle to Marty. "If it was *my* son, I hope I'd have the guts."

They start lining up now, crowding around him.

"After all you did for him . . . all you gave him . . ."

"Selling heroin to rich kids to make money for bombs . . ."

"Who did he think he was? Some goddam Robin Hood?"

"Bernie the Bandit—even when he was little . . ."

"Thank you very much," Marty tells them. "I did what I had to . . . what I felt in my heart . . ."

"You taught him a lesson he'll never forget . . ."

"Think they can hurt people and still be loved . . ."

"Remember me?" says an arthritic old lady, gnarled and rouged, in white anklets.

"Aunt Beatrice. How *are* you?" Marty says.

"How can I be? Whatever I get falls from my sister's chin."

"Call Howard tomorrow. Tell him what you need."

"God bless you," she says, and kisses his hand.

"Who did you teach a lesson this morning?" Danny's turn now, drunk and loud.

Marty looks at him without flinching. "I had to answer some questions about this sabotage in Texas."

"What do *you* know about it?"

"One of Bernie's accomplices is still on the loose. They think the kid behind this may be the same man."

"It's all in their heads," Danny tells him. "Just

before I left, the Rangers were rounding up Chicanos, forcing them at gunpoint to take out their *peckeritos* just in case one of them might be this Jewish Maoist you're talking about cleverly disguised as the Cisco Kid."

"Everybody's a suspect," Marty says. "Even *you*."

"Danny?" Betty says.

"Why not?" Marty tells her. "He's Bernie's cousin, isn't he? He did leave town in a hurry. Even this kid you took movies of," he says to Danny, "the ones they showed me—of this Ricardo Perez—he *worked* for you, didn't he? As a part-time caddy and stud."

"What movies?" Joe says.

"We put on a little show one night," Danny answers, his voice tight, his eyes cold on Marty. "At the anti-war coffeehouse in town. Ricardo played a faggot Ranger with a red, white and blue Stetson and a sawed-off shotgun between his legs."

Somebody laughs.

"The FBI thought the movies I took that night might come in handy. And if I didn't want Ricardo to know who I was working for, I should turn them over."

"You did the right thing," Marty says. "Your friend Ricardo just might be blackmailing homosexual officers into committing sabotage."

"Sounds just like my screenplay," Danny laughs. Then, with a fag lisp, to Gloria, Howard's honey-hair: "Wanna hear how I helped Ricardo Perez whose real name is Myron Putz slip poison gas into a shipment of spray deodorant headed for PX's all over the world?"

"Same old Danny," Howard says.

"Father-sucker," Danny mutters.

Betty starts another parade. Of strawberry cheesecake. Strawberry short. Cannoli, napoleons, ice cream for sundaes. I squirt, Amy scoops, as they make their way across the room—spilling coffee, balancing plates, dripping hot fudge, squashing cherries. Betty comes over and says what's so funny? I wipe whipped cream off the tip of her nose.

"Where's Peter?" she asks Amy.

"Inside—with my mother."

"Your mother's over there."

"He must be with Danny."

We look and call for him.

"Some mother," Betty whispers. "Doesn't know where her child is."

I go into my room and find Peter in the closet, Danny kissing honey-hair inside the door.

"Well, look who's here," Danny says. "Nick meet Gloria. Gloria, this is Nick. You're in his tie rack."

"Hi," she smiles.

"I was looking for Peter."

"Peter? Peter who? You mean my son?" Danny says. "How considerate of you to be concerned for his whereabouts."

"Did you find him?" Betty calls.

"In here," I answer.

"What's everybody doing in the closet?" she asks.

"Getting acquainted," Danny says.

She picks Peter up. "Where did you go, you naughty boy? Grandma saved a charlotte rousse—just for you."

"What about me?" Danny says.

"*You* have lipstick on your mouth."

"Where else should it be?"

"Wipe it off," she orders. "Before your wife comes in."

Danny smiles. And wipes. With one of the ties.

Betty slaps it out of his hand.

"What's the matter?" he says. "It's one of *mine*, isn't it?"

Trembling, she shields the baby and takes him from the room.

"Anybody for a charlotte rousse?" Danny says.

Gloria laughs and slides out between us.

"Fine girl, Gloria. Maybe she can squeeze you in between me and Marty." He smiles. "Or are you getting all you need? Here at home?"

I'm about to tell him when Amy walks in.

"Your Uncle Barney's leaving," she says. "He's offered us a lift."

"I'm talking to Nick," he tells her.

"My mother can't take much more," she says.

"Neither can I," he laughs. "*You* go—and take your mother with you."

She clenches her fists.

"I can't stop," he says later, drunk and groggy, when we're all cleaned up, alone in the living room.

Joe and Betty are asleep.

"It's always like this when my work isn't going well."

He closes his eyes.

"You and my mother want to fuck, that's your—and my father's—problem," he says, smiling. "The first time *I* cheated, a week after the honeymoon, I got this terrific boil on the back of my neck—it took all I had not to become a religious fanatic."

He laughs. "That's *my* problem. I still believe people *pay* for their sins."

He opens his eyes.

"You don't talk much, do you?"

"I've got nothing to say."

We look at each other.

"I should have been Marty's son," he says, closing his eyes again.

I wait for him to go on. He doesn't. We sit there a long time.

"I should go home," he says, finally, without moving. Then, getting up, he stumbles and I catch him.

"It won't be easy—killing you," he says.

I help him. Into his old bed.

9

I left.

Not by choice.

He got rid of me.

The first week after the party I started delivering fish to his apartment on Amsterdam Avenue in the nineties. One of Joe's best customers had moved to Central Park West, so every Wednesday when I biked that delivery over I'd drop filet off at Amy and Danny's in time for the baby's lunch.

The apartment was a mess. He still hadn't put up any shelves so there were cartons all over the place with Peter getting into all of them, pulling out books, toys, breaking knic-knacks.

Amy's mother was in her room, sleeping.

Danny was in a sweat.

"How's the screenplay?" I ask stupidly, over a cup of coffee.

"Terrific," he says. "Wanna read it?"

He pulls out a yellow page from his typewriter on the kitchen table and hands it to me.

There's nothing on it.

"I've got a whole ream inside. Terrific as that one."

"If you could just get organized," Amy tells him, "and build a desk."

"Where?" he snaps. "In your mother's room?"

"Ours," she says. "And lock the door."

Peter takes out pots and pans.

"You could use *my* room," I holler, over his banging.

They both look at me.

"Nobody's home," I say. "We're all at the store."

He took me up on it.

We never saw him, though. He'd arrive after we'd leave, and leave before we'd get home. The way the room looked, you'd never even know he was there.

"He's here and he's not here," Betty said. "Like living with a ghost."

By July, she was getting edgier every day. Some nights she didn't even come in to say good night. Then one night, when she did, "just talk to me," she said.

We lay there in silence listening to Joe's breathing.

"He's sick," she whispers. "All week he's been complaining of a bad taste . . ."

"Do you think he knows about us?" I ask.

"He's not that good an actor." She laughs.

I rub her belly.

"It's the money," she says, out of nowhere. "All of a sudden it's like it never happened. Like it never will."

I move my hand inside her crotch.

"What's the matter with you?" she says, taking my hand away. "Can't you just have a conversation?"

Then out of nowhere again: "Where will we go?"

I look at her. "When?"

"When the check comes through. You don't think I'm going to stay here, do you?"

"What about Peter? Danny?"

"I'm not going to think about it," she says. "Why? Don't you want to come with me?"

"Sure," I shrug, staring at the ceiling.

She takes my hand and returns it to where it was.

"There's something wrong with you," she says. "A young boy should go out—with girls."

It was time to leave.

The next day, just before we close, this blonde comes in to buy shrimps, and I realize it's the one with the valuables, the one I split the chicken with.

Ducking behind the board, I get busy scraping.

Then just when I think she hasn't recognized me, she walks over and smiles: "I didn't mind your taking the TV," she says, "but the ballpoint was a present and what the hell do you do with one slipper?"

Joe and Betty look up, like fish, with their mouths open.

The blonde looks at me like maybe she should call a cop, but then she just laughs and shrugs and goes out with her shrimps.

"I never saw her before," I tell them.

But that night I can hear them whispering and later when Betty comes in she wants to know how come I don't ever call my mother and where did I live before *exactly* and why don't I have any friends.

The TV is on so I just keep watching. "A hundred and tenth Street," I tell her. "My friends are in Canada . . . Or Vietnam . . . Some I don't want to see anymore. . . ."

Then just when she's about to throw me another, Chris Baker comes on with the news again, this time from Ciudad Juarez, Mexico.

"The FBI cracked open the San Lorenzo, Texas, sabotage case today," Chris tells us, "with the arrest here of fleeing suspect Ricardo Perez, a twenty-two-year-old Mexican-American charged with blackmailing an Air Force officer into sabotaging a parachute drop of tanks and tractors last May resulting in the deaths of a dozen schoolchildren."

Ricardo Perez shields his face as the FBI leads him, handcuffed, through reporters and flashbulbs.

"After a month of intensive search and interrogation, FBI agents found a highly personal and revealing diary belonging to the officer in a secret pocket of Perez's golf bag. The golf bag was a gift to Perez from the officer's wife for being their best caddy. . . ."

Flashes of golf bag. Wife. Officer. Their kids.

"The officer, Colonel Barnes Johnson, a decorated Korean War hero, was found dead from shotgun wounds last night, an apparent suicide . . ."

When the phone rings, we both get it.

"They stole it," Danny screams on the other end.

"What does it mean?" Betty asks.

"They stole my screenplay idea, *that's* what it means . . . and they're going to nail Ricardo. . . ."

"Is he innocent?" I ask.

"It's all a frame-up."

"How do *you* know?" Betty says. "How well do you know him?"

"I was his *pimp*, remember?"

The next night Danny was on a plane to Texas. Expenses paid.

He stayed for three days.

In the meantime, I delivered fish to Amy and the baby. And helped them to get organized.

"Don't they need you at the store?" Amy asked.

"It's summer," I tell her. "Business is slow."

"Where *were* you?" Betty asks when I get back.

"Amy needed help," I tell her. "I put up some shelves."

I even went over in the evenings so that, by the time Danny returned, the place was all cleaned up.

"You really move in and get things done, don't you?" he says, coming home to find me there, shirtless and sweaty, with Peter on my lap, a beer and paint brush in my hands. "If you think *this* is hot, you should have been in Texas."

"What happened?" Amy asks him. "Why did they keep you so long?"

"They ask a lot of questions," he says. "And put a lot of words in your mouth."

He looks exhausted, like he hasn't slept.

"The whole case depends on the diary they found in Ricardo's golf bag," he says, sitting down and putting his head back. Amy gets him a beer. "Ricardo says he didn't even know the diary was there. That somebody planted it."

"Who?" I ask. "The FBI?"

"The colonel's wife, maybe. Ricardo says one night when they were in bed, she showed him the diary and said wouldn't it be fun to hide it and scare the colonel out of his wits."

"What's in the diary?" Amy asks.

"The colonel's fantasies," Danny answers. "Mostly homosexual. About Ricardo."

He takes a sip of beer.

"I *know* Lois Johnson, the colonel's wife," he says sarcastically. "I wouldn't put it past her. Ricardo says she must have slipped the diary in that night when she gave him the golf bag as a present."

"So then it's all a coincidence and Ricardo wasn't blackmailing the colonel at all."

Danny laughs. "Tell *that* to the FBI."

"Why did Johnson kill himself?" Amy asks.

"They found his diary, didn't they? The poor bastard *knew* they would use it. They *had* to—to make their case."

Peter starts to get fidgety and eat the paint brush. I pull it away and he starts to cry.

"He's hot," Amy says. "I'll put him to bed."

"How's your mother?" Danny asks her.

"In pain," she says. "I think she'll have to go to the hospital." She takes Peter inside.

"Just what I need," Danny says. "And how's *our* mother?" he smiles.

It got hotter.

With Amy's mother in the hospital, Amy was there almost every day, leaving Peter with Danny who gave him to Betty, leaving Danny free to work at *his* place.

He *ate* at ours.

"Your mother won't remember what a fish smells like," Joe says to Danny one night over dinner. "You better hurry up with that screenplay so I can have her back where she belongs."

"I'm really into it now," Danny smiles, like he's trying to sell us something. But then another night he tells us Nichols called and that they want a first draft by the first of August.

"What's his hurry?" Betty asks.

"If they make the movie, they want to do it right away," Danny explains. "To cash in—on this Texas thing."

"So?" Joe says. "You're *into* it, aren't you?"

"Sure," Danny smiles. "But I'm not a machine."

"It's no use," he whispers later when they go inside. "The whole thing is falling apart."

"What's wrong?" I ask him.

He shrugs. "Amy's mother is worse. They're operating again tomorrow. But they don't think it'll do any good."

"Can I help?"

He laughs. "Would you like to write my movie for me, too?"

The next morning, Amy's mother died on the operating table. She was cremated the same day.

"I have nobody to talk to now," Amy says quietly, almost to herself, when we're at the chapel.

Joe and Betty took care of all the expenses.

August first, Danny was back in my room still

working on *Public Spectacle*. "They've given me till the fifteenth," he said.

August *fourteenth,* we got the call. Peter had suffered convulsions, Danny told us, and had beaten himself unconscious against his crib.

"Just a few minor bruises," Danny reported. "The heat brought it on. And fever from a sore throat. We don't have to worry it'll happen again."

"He's not telling me something," Betty whispers that night. "He's always confided in me. I know when he's holding back."

The next call was for me.

"Don't say anything," Amy says, reaching me at the store. "Pretend I'm a customer."

"Salmon? Yes, we have fresh salmon," I tell her.

"I have to see you," she says. "You're the only one I can trust."

"Two-ninety a pound."

"Meet me at Ninety-sixth and Central Park West. In a half hour."

"Where you going?" Betty asks me.

"I gotta bike this over," I tell her. "The lady wants it before three."

Amy's waiting when I get there. With Peter asleep and bandaged, in the stroller.

"It wasn't convulsions," she says.

"I know," I tell her.

She looks at me and her eyes fill with tears.

"Let's walk," she says.

I push the bike. She pushes the stroller.

"The baby was up that night. Screaming," she says. "Danny was trying to work. When he gave Peter the bottle and Peter flung it at him, Danny picked him up and started banging him against the crib."

"Where were you?"

"On sleeping pills," she says. "I've been on them since my mother died."

An old bum comes over and walks beside us.

"What are you going to do?" I ask her.

"Get away, I guess."

"Where?" the bum asks her.

We stop and look at him.

"I don't know," she laughs, sobbing at the same time.

The bum gets scared and scurries away.

We sit on a bench.

"I'll give you money," I tell her. "Take Peter—on a plane."

"I have no family," she says.

"Neither do I. I'll come with you."

She looks at me and smiles.

I pet her face.

It was all set. My savings came to $850. By September first, an even thousand. Amy, Peter, and me. All we had to do was pick a place.

But then Betty came in and said, "I spoke to Danny. I found out what really happened."

"What?" I ask her.

"At first, he wouldn't tell me. But then I got it out of him. It was Amy," she says. "She hasn't been herself since her mother died. Peter was sick that night. Screaming with fever. She couldn't take it. Danny woke up and found her beating him—against the crib."

"That's not true," I tell her.

"How do *you* know?" she says.

"Amy told me."

"Told you what? When?"

"The other day. I met her in the park."

"On whose time? Yours or ours?"

"It was Danny who beat Peter."

"Who says so? Her? What do you want her to say?"

"I believe her. And so do you."

"That's a lie," she says, and holds back from hitting me.

"We're going to take Peter away from her," she says, finally.

"You're crazy."

"I'm calling my brother Marty tomorrow. He'll tell us what to do."

Marty told them they needed evidence.

"Don't worry," I told Amy. "They have nothing on you."

But then Joe came in one night with Betty behind him and said, "We have something to show you."

He threads the tape and turns on the TV.

Only instead of Danny, it's Nick-and-Amy Time now—pushing Peter in his stroller down Central Park West. Even the bum got in. And for a fade-out, Amy's smile—as I stroke her face.

"Danny!" I yell out. "And his zoom lens."

"That's not all," Betty says, turning on the light. "Three nights—when Danny was in Texas—*putting up bookshelves*," she says sarcastically. "In your underwear, the neighbor says—in front of the baby—with the poor mother dying in the next room."

"Oh my God."

"Fish deliveries that took all afternoon."

"Don't let them do this," I beg Joe.

"Not to mention an affidavit by her physician confirming her despondency, her dependence on pills."

I shake my head.

"Where did you *get* this?" she asks suddenly, picking up my pen, the ballpoint, from my desk.

"I bought it," I tell her.

"Fourteen-karat gold? You didn't buy it since you're working for us," she says. "Who was that woman?"

"What woman?"

"The woman who came into the store. Who accused you of stealing."

"I told you. I never saw her before."

We look at each other.

"Danny's testifying that every Wednesday when he came home from work and you had been there, he smelled fish in his bed," she says.

I sit down.

"We're slapping a temporary injunction on Amy tomorrow, taking the baby away immediately."

I look at Joe.

"Pack up," he says.

10

We switched places.

Danny got his room back and I moved in with Amy.

It didn't make any difference what the neighbors saw or thought anymore. If we were lovers, okay. Danny was dangerous, out of his mind. We were going to prove Amy *had* to come to me for help.

All I had to do was get back in that room and find his tape—"the crazy one" he sent to Betty by mistake.

"There'll be other tapes," Amy said. "He made them all the time."

Our plan was to keep watch, then go upstairs when nobody was home.

They left a key under the mat for the cleaning

woman on Thursday mornings. If I got there by seven thirty, I could beat her to it.

Thursday was a week away.

So we took turns and watched. From the playground across the street.

Betty left at seven. Without me there, she had to get to the store early—back on her old schedule. Over the weekend, Danny didn't appear at all.

"What does he do up there all day?" Amy asks me.

"Work on his screenplay, I guess."

"There is no more screenplay," she tells me.

I look at her, scared.

"They wouldn't extend his deadline," she says. "And what he *did* send them, they didn't like."

"Oh Jesus."

Monday, Danny came down with the baby. I followed two blocks behind as he pushed the stroller to the bakery, then to the playground where he watched a hockey game and ate from a bag. Whatever was inside, he couldn't get enough of it. Then two men came over and sat down next to him, one on each side. They talked for a while and then the men went away. Danny seemed upset, agitated. He started eating again, then quickly got up and pushed Peter home.

Tuesday and Wednesday, he didn't come out again. Then Thursday morning, I stole the key.

"Danny won't know it's gone," I tell Amy on the phone, downstairs, on the corner. "He'll just let the cleaning woman in and think Betty forgot to leave it."

"But *they'll* know," she says, "when it isn't there tonight—back under the mat."

I had to move fast.

"Hello?" Danny says, when I call him later from the same booth, after the cleaning woman leaves for the day.

"I want to talk to you," I tell him. "This is Nick."

"What about?"

"If you want to keep Peter you'd better meet me at the UN at five thirty."

Soon as they're off in a taxi, I go upstairs.

Only the tapes aren't there. I look all over but all I can find are Betty's. I even take apart some of Peter's toys. Then only when he's at the door and I'm in the closet do I realize he must have them with him.

He *does* have them. I can *see* them—through the crack in the closet—when he comes into the room with Peter and gives him his bottle and they fall out —of Peter's diaper bag.

"Your Uncle Nick is up to something," he tells Peter, picking the tapes up. "Wouldn't they just love to get a hold of *these*?"

He stops, as if he's just figured out why I called him, and looks around. "They wouldn't dare," he smiles. "They're not that smart."

He looks around again—in my direction.

"Still," he says. "We better keep these hidden. I can't take them everywhere," he laughs, and puts them where I can't see.

"You won't tell anybody now, will you?" he says to Peter.

I can hear Peter sucking on his bottle.

"Of course not," Danny says. "You're Daddy's buddy, aren't you?"

He picks Peter up, back in my sight again.

"They want *me* to talk," he says. "But I won't . . ."

He hugs Peter close, stroking his hair.

Peter starts to cry.

"What's the matter? Daddy loves you," Danny says. "He won't hurt you . . . I know. Let's make another movie. . . ."

He puts Peter down and sets things up.

"You be me and I'll be the FBI."

Peter starts sucking again.

"You vant to go to jail?" Danny asks him in a shrill Gestapo. "The colonel's vife says she *paid* you for Ricardo's services. You know vat *zat* makes you, don't you? Now I vill give you von more chance . . . Did you or did you not ever see zis diary before? . . . Come now . . . *Think . . . Remember . . .*"

"Don't *let* me . . . don't *let* me talk," he pleads with Peter suddenly, in his own voice.

Peter starts to cry again.

"What did you do, you naughty boy? . . . You *stink*," he cries out.

Then: "Sssh . . . I won't tell on you . . . You don't tell on me . . . Come, my little stink-shad. . . . We'll take a bath. . . ."

When the water's running, I make a dash for it. And throw the key under the mat.

That weekend I took Amy to the country. It was no use sticking around. Danny wouldn't do anything crazy with Betty and Joe home. Monday, I'd start keeping watch again, and Thursday, I'd get those tapes.

We rented a car and drove up the New York Thruway into farm country where we followed an old roller-coaster back road right into somebody's driveway. The somebody didn't seem to be home, so we got out and called and when there was no answer we went up and peeked in and everything was covered with sheets and newspapers. Snooping around, we found an old tree swing, and a garden, and a 1938 Hudson station wagon, dead, in the garage.

The garden had scallions, so we pulled them out and ate them as we walked up a high hill through rotted apples and birch trees, picking Queen Anne's lace.

It was one of those hot early September afternoons, so we took our sweaters off and kept walking till we came to a big pond with a race-track bench at its edge and catfish who wiggled to the surface to frown and stare at us every time I skimmed it with a pebble.

"Do you think they'd mind if we jumped in?"

"You first," Amy smiles.

When we're both in, a dog appears, jumping and barking like the pond is his.

"What's the idea?" says an old guy, behind him, toothless, with glasses, in torn overalls.

"Nobody was around," I tell him. "It's a hot day."

He gives us a look and then says, "You married?"

"We married?" I ask Amy.

"Sure," she tells him. "Come on in."

The old guy laughs and tells the dog to shut up. "You're in his pool," he says to us. "He comes up here every hour to cool off after chasing rabbits."

The dog jumps in and shakes himself off.

"I guess it's okay—if you're married," the old guy says. "The owner's wife died last month. That's why he's not here. I look after the place for him. They call me Pop."

"What's the dog's name?" Amy asks.

"Dog," the old guy tells her. "If you give me your names, we'll send you a Christmas card."

I give him our names and address.

"There used to be a wife," he says, "but like the owner's, she died."

Then just to me: "We gotta learn to look after ourselves, you know."

Dog is off again, chasing rabbits.

"Don't let the catfish bite you," the old guy laughs.

When he's gone and I'm drying Amy's back with my sweater, I kiss her on the neck.

She turns around.

"It's painful—being alive again," she says.

I kiss her mouth.

"Danny says I have a funny smell."

"Scallions," I tell her.

"No, I mean it. When I was nursing the baby, he couldn't stand to come near me."

I kiss her again.

"It's not all his fault," she says. "I said terrible things to him. One night when some friends came over and they asked how his screenplay was coming and he said terrific, I said tell them the truth, why don't you? And he just got up and walked out. Then about a week later, when we were in bed and he rejected me, I said: 'Faggot . . . Mama's boy . . . You make me feel like a whore . . . a nymphomaniac . . .' when all I really wanted was to touch him, for him to touch me. . . ."

"It's all over now," I tell her.

"I was jealous," she says. "Even when it drove him crazy, he had his work. While I had nothing—not even my mother anymore—just his baby—*their* baby, his mother's and his."

I kiss her cheek, her eyes.

"I miss my mother," she says. "Last night I dreamed about her again. In a beautiful party dress. I was on the telephone, laughing, and she wanted to hear. She put her ear next to mine, but it was no use . . ."

"I love you," I whisper. "I want to take care of you."

"Too painful," she repeats.

I spread out the sweater.

Gently, then violently, we give death a ride for its money.

Monday I followed Danny to the bakery again, only instead of taking Peter to the playground, he goes to a small deserted neighborhood park across the street from a schoolyard and sits there awhile until this dark Spanish-looking kid comes along in tight jeans and a polo shirt. The kid bends down to admire Peter and pretty soon he and Danny are sharing the bakery bag. Another ten minutes, and I'm following them home.

Tight Jeans doesn't come down again till almost six.

That night, when Amy asks me if I saw Danny, I tell her no.

Tuesday, Tight Jeans arrives early—with a girl this time who looks like his sister. They go upstairs and stay all day.

Wednesday, the same story.

Thursday morning, I steal the key again. Then, no sooner does the cleaning woman go up when she's downstairs again and back on the bus.

Around twelve, Tight Jeans and Sis show up. About a half hour behind them, the two men who upset Danny in the playground last week.

They're all upstairs now.

Tight Jeans and Sis are out in twenty minutes.

The two men—an hour later.

It's almost two. I call Amy and tell her I've got the key—if Danny doesn't come down by five, *she's* going to call him this time and tell him he's got to meet her, that the FBI's been asking all sorts of questions.

Four thirty, Danny comes running out. His eyes wild, his shirt open and wet.

No Peter.

I don't know whether to run after Danny or go upstairs.

I go up.

The key's unnecessary. The door's open.

Instead of going into the room with the tapes, I follow the running water.

Peter's in the tub, face down.

I try to save him, but it's too late.

Panicking, I run out and look for Danny.

A woman comes up and says what's the matter?

Terrible accident. Ten K.

She stands there frightened. I run up the block. No Danny. Anywhere. I run into a phone booth. Joe answers. I scream COME HOME.

By the time I get back, the police are there. I tell them who I am . . . I used to live here . . . I came back to get something . . . Found Peter drowned . . .

Betty. Joe. Both at once.

Peter's in the bathroom covered with a towel.

Betty collapses. Joe gets sick.

They hold me for questioning till the call about Danny. Dead. Subway. Crushed. Train.

The room spins, shattered by screams.

I tell Amy about Peter when she's in my arms.

11

Chris Baker had the full story: "A sworn statement signed by a former television comic just before he committed suicide in New York last week could help to send a young anarchist to the electric chair, FBI sources disclosed today. . . ."

A picture of Danny fills the television screen—a smiling one from his wall.

"Danny Dime, the comic and screenwriter, who jumped to his death in front of an oncoming subway train last Thursday, apparently despondent over the accidental drowning of his ten-month-old son, was a friend and former employer of Ricardo Perez, the young Mexican-American Brown Power activist accused of sabotaging Organization Cleansweep, the mock war exercise in San Lorenzo, Texas, which has taken almost thirty lives . . ."

A picture of Ricardo now.

"Since his arrest in this bizarre case, Perez has charged that the Air Force colonel's diary found in his golf bag, which he allegedly stole for blackmail purposes, was planted there by either the FBI or Mrs. Barnes Johnson, the colonel's wife. . . ."

Picture of wife.

"According to Dime's statement, however, the comic came upon the diary last May and asked Perez what it was. '*Fairy*-tales,' Perez allegedly winked and told him, 'which are going to make a lot of little brown children very happy . . .' The killing of a dozen *white* children by a parachute drop of tanks and tractors occurred a few days later. . . ."

More of Danny on the other channels and in the morning papers, smiling, like he's finally made it.

Joe calls the next night.

"I want to see you," he says, having trouble breathing. "Come to the house."

"What for?" I ask him.

"Please," he says. "Betty's at her brother's."

When I get there, the apartment is dark. Joe's unshaven, in his slippers, a hundred years older. He doesn't say anything. He just looks at me like he's drugged and lets me in. I follow him into Danny's room and he turns on the tape-machine.

"Sit down," he says.

He sits next to me—where Betty used to sit—and Amy appears, under the dryer, nursing the baby.

"There are some things you can do nothing about," Danny reminds us, invisible, like he's talking from the grave now.

I ask Joe where he found it.

"I was cleaning things out," he answers hoarsely, his eyes dead on the screen. "It fell out—from one of Peter's toys."

We watch the rest of it, only instead of ending where it did, there's more now.

Danny, in bed, naked, Amy asleep, with her back to him, as he sits there fondling himself.

"Even when it's good. . . ." he tells us. Amy stirs and turns over. He stops and waits.

"Even when it's good—like tonight—I need something else. . . ."

Danny and Amy making love. Amy suddenly pulls away and says, "I'm sorry, I can't."

"Shit," Danny says, and turns his back on her.

"It's like we're putting on a show," she says. "Like you want me to perform."

"Forget it," he tells her and flicks it off.

"I just came in to be neighborly," a woman tells us in a deep southern drawl. "Who would have dreamed I'd be making a movie?"

She's sitting on a sofa in a curly blue Marie Antoinette shower cap, her breasts like overgrown peaches bunched up over the opening in her robe. Danny comes into the picture and sits beside her.

"I just wanted to apologize for Merde waking you up every morning," she says. "I keep telling her to take the garbage around the back and burn it, but she's afraid of fire, poor child, so she keeps leaving it at your doorstep instead."

Danny smiles and puts his arm around her.

"Merde's really a good little girl," the woman goes on, blinking, smiling. "I found her name in a novel when she was still in my tum-tum. Pretty, don't you think?"

Danny kisses her neck.

She goes on, blinking, smiling.

"I love pretty things. Sometimes I call up real-estate agents and pretend I'm in the market for a house just so I can get inside one and see how other people live. . . ."

Danny kisses her breasts.

She goes on, blinking, smiling.

"Bathrooms are the best . . ."

He slips his hand between her legs.

"I love flowered toilet paper, don't you?"

He slips off her robe.

"They didn't have flowered toilet paper when I was a girl," she goes on, blinking, smiling. "What I really love is when the people aren't home so I can just imagine them . . ."

He removes her brassiere.
"People are so cruel, don't you think?"
He bites her nipple.
"You're not cruel, though, *are* you?"
She blinks and smiles.

Amy's mother, sleeping, Danny's voice, quietly: "You have cancer. And I don't love your daughter . . ."
She opens her eyes and squints.
"Danny? . . . Is that you? . . . What are you doing with the camera?"
"You looked just like Amy," he answers, and bends over to kiss her.

"No wonder your wife isn't enough for you. You don't give her a chance . . ."
Another woman now. The colonel's wife. Straddling, screwing him.
"Like my husband," she says. "Always *doing* things. Afraid to surrender. To let *me* fuck *him*."
She laughs. And picks up speed.
"How do you like being fucked for a change?"

Monkey—in a zoo cage—rubbing his erection while two of his cronies explore each other's assholes.
"They kept looking at me in the cafeteria while I was feeding Peter . . ."

Two men stand there laughing, throwing peanuts at the monkey.

"Two fags," Danny tells us, voiced-over. "The more they looked, the more I performed: Loving Father. All-American. Kissing Peter. Talking baby-talk . . ."

The monkey shrieks, baring his gums.

"I'm going to do something terrible," Danny warns us. "In the meantime, I take movies. And straighten pictures. . . ."

Peter, on the floor, crying, frightened. Danny's voice, muffled and whispered:

"Come on, you little fuck . . . This is Hide and Seek. Daddy's hiding in the bathtub . . . Try and find him . . ."

Danny laughs. Peter screams.

Peter, on the floor, banging cymbals, Danny, masturbating with Peter's panda.

Young man. Smiling. He looks familiar. Dark. Handsome. Ricardo Perez.

"You little man, Danny. You worry everybody think you have small cock. . . ."

Gary Cooper. And Charles Laughton. On TV. In an old movie.

Laughton to Cooper: "To look like you must be a happy thing . . ."

Ricardo, smiling, holding vase of flowers.
"You look worried," he says. "I won't drop it."
"It's Amy's," Danny answers, edgy, off-camera.
Ricardo shrugs. "You would buy her another."
"It's one of a kind. It belonged to her family."
"Then she would have to learn—to live without it."

Danny, in close-up, meeting our eyes:
"Dreaming of Ricardo, I wake in terror . . . the neighbor next door—coughing my guts up—like we're both connected by the same intestine . . . Fingered into orgasm, Amy's asleep . . . I get out of bed . . . Driven . . . Hungry . . . I have to have it. Hard. Up the ass . . . Kitchen. Banana. Too soft. Disgusting. No pleasure. Hurts. I put it next to me. Curved. Hung-over. I stroke and squeeze it. Splitting the skin. Slipping inside it. Cock. Pussy. Both at once. Mess. Shame. Cold. Silly. . . ."

Danny, screaming, at his face in the mirror: "You don't want freedom. You want relief!"

Danny, on his knees, before open toilet bowl: "Dear God. Help me. I can't be one thing. . . ."

Amy, asleep, Danny, whimpering: "I can't help it. You stink . . . You stink. . . ."

Danny, trembling, holding the vase. He lets it drop. It smashes to pieces.

Colonel's wife. Wearing dildo. Fucking Danny. Up the ass.

"Hello, darling. Meet Nick . . ."
Betty's voice. Me. On tape. Standing there, smiling. Being introduced.
"He walked into our store and we took him home with us. Isn't he handsome? You should see him work. . . ."

Danny, holding puppet, doing show for Peter: "Hello. My name's Nick . . ."
He turns the puppet around. It has another face.
"Hello. My name's Rick . . ."
He turns it again, back and forth.
"Nickie . . . Rickie . . . Nicardo . . . Ricardo. . . ."

Girl doll this time. With red curly hair:
"See Nana eat the banana?"
He stuffs a banana in the doll's face.

Colonel's wife. Wearing dildo. Danny on his knees. Between her legs.

Bette Davis. In an old movie. Telling her husband she can't wait for him to die.

Same movie. The husband collapses. Bette sits there—as he gropes for his medicine.

Danny, screaming. Fucking colonel's wife. Slapping, punching her, pulling her hair.

Amy, asleep, Peter sleeping beside her, Danny's voice, hushed and tired:
"Dear God. Stop me. Before it's too late . . ."

A bat, flying around a room.

Danny, sitting, staring at his typewriter. No paper in the roller. The typewriter, humming.

The bat, circling, around and around.

Gloria, smiling, looking into camera, as Danny kisses, feels, undresses her.

Betty and Joe—smiling from the wall.

Home movie: Joe—in the old days—standing in the window of Paddy's Restaurant—big hat and apron—boning shad. The camera moves in on his fast fingers.

Danny's typewriter, still. A long close-up.

Danny's picture—his graduation—smiling, happy, his arms around his parents.
Danny's voice—as he pans along the wall:
"They want me to cooperate . . . to say I saw the diary . . ."
The camera stops at Danny as a boy scout, fat and funny-looking, saluting the flag.

Danny and Gloria, going at it violently. Amy walks in, carrying bundles . . . Gloria gasps, ducks under the covers.
Danny smiling, to Amy: "I *did* the dishes . . ."

Amy asleep, Danny's voice:
"You can't hurt me now, she said, her mother lying there. So cold. So dead. So final. So real . . ."

Danny, in close-up, meeting our eyes again: "Last night—by the river—I took a walk. Even now I'm not sure. I may have dreamed it . . . A woman. Standing there . . . Ready to jump. She looks at me, coldly. I've interrupted her. I want to apologize . . . tell her I'm sorry . . . She laughs, like she knows me, and stares back at the river. I walk on, quickly, till I hear the smack: body hitting water. I stop, paralyzed. No sound. No struggle. Complete surrender. No last-second wish to save her life . . .

I stand there, terrified . . . jealous . . . thrilled . . . Run back. No sign. No sound. Just the river. Somewhere underneath—our sweet secret . . ."

Peter banging at Danny's typewriter.
Danny's voice: "Idea for a story . . . Loving father wants to kill his child. One day in the playground a madman pulls a knife. The child is butchered. The father takes revenge . . ."

Peter, asleep, his head bandaged.
Danny standing there over his crib: "The terrible thing is I know what I'm doing. Killing the child in myself who won't let me grow up . . ."
He bends down close to Peter's ear:
"I'm sorry . . . Forgive me . . . I'll make it up to you . . ."

Danny—as a kid—another home movie—dancing, clowning, making faces.

Danny—in a corner—crouched and sniveling: "She said it was Amy's fault . . . I let her believe it. . . . I wanted to tell her . . . but she made me lie . . ."

A blond girl doll with a broken neck. Nickie-Rickie flung on top of her. Danny bends down cheek-to-cheek with the Nana doll:

"That'll teach you to stink up my bed."

Danny and Peter. Playing FBI. That day I watched them from inside the closet.
"I won't tell on you . . . You don't tell on me . . . Come, my little stink-shad . . . We'll take a bath . . ."

"You're all I have," Danny says to Peter. "This morning when I shaved I tried to grab the water. YOU CAN'T GRAB WATER!" Danny shouts, picking Peter up, squeezing, shaking him.

Danny, in rocker, holding Peter, stroking the dildo between his legs.
"You're going to tell on me, I know. As soon as you can talk . . ."

Betty and Danny, cheek-to-cheeking on the wall.
Danny's voice: "You tricked . . . deceived me . . . To quiet the silence, you kept me talking. In the name of trust, you took away my secrets . . ."

Peter asleep, Danny pacing.
"They want a statement. Next week—or else . . ."

Danny, screaming at Rickie-Nickie:
"*I* stole the diary . . . *I* killed those kids . . ."

Tight Jeans, naked, on Joe and Betty's bed. Danny down on him, Peter watching.

Peter eating chocolate, making a mess. Danny's voice as he feeds him more: "You won't tell on me . . . I won't tell on you . . ."

Tight Jeans and Sis. Danny, watching. Peter on his lap, eating chocolate.

Danny and Sis. As Tight Jeans sits there, bouncing Peter—up and down on his foot.

Danny, Sis, and Tight Jeans. Peter, screaming. The men from the playground walk in and surprise them.

Rickie-Nickie—propped up in a chair. Danny puts a hood on him, sets him afire.

Danny posed, like the Statue of Liberty, draped in a sheet, the dildo for a torch.

Peter eating chocolate, Danny slapping him.
"Come on, you little fuck. Say your first word. What's it gonna be? Informer? Cock-sucker? Let's hear it—for Grandma and Grandpa . . ."
Peter wails. Danny clutches him.

"I'm sorry . . . I'm sorry . . ."

He starts to cry.

"But you have no right to be my judge . . ."

Suddenly. Panicked: "What did you do? . . . Grandma's bed . . . All dirty . . ."

He rubs at it furiously, his hands get messy.

"I'm going to have to punish you, you naughty boy . . . Wash your mouth out with soap . . . for telling stories . . ."

He takes Peter out of the picture. We sit there watching the smiling wall. Then the sound of water filling the tub. Peter's cries, suddenly stopped.

"Turn it off," Joe says.

Danny runs back, stares at us in horror, reaches out, covers the lens.

I turn it off. Joe sits there.

"Get me water," he says.

I run into the kitchen. When I come back, he takes a pill.

I stand there over him a long time. As he catches his breath, winces in pain.

"I got the money," he finally says. "I'm leaving Sunday. Come with me . . ."

"Where?" I ask him.

"Wherever you say. We'll open our restaurant. Just the two of us . . ."

"I can't," I tell him.
"Why not?"
"Amy," I answer.
He shakes his head.
"Has Betty seen this?"
"Tomorrow," he says.
"Are you sure?" I ask.
"I hope it kills her."

I sit beside him, put my hand on his. He starts to weep, I put my arm around him.

When I get up, he says: "You can bring Amy with you."

"I'll talk to her," I tell him. "I'll let you know...."

Betty's call came the next night.
"Meet me at the store. I have to see you."
"About what?" I ask her.
"Please . . ." she begs.

The store is dark, the walls empty. Only the fishnet hanging from the ceiling.

"He showed you these to punish me," Betty says at the sink. Danny's tapes are burning slowly.

"They stink," she says. We watch them smoke. Disintegrate.

"I have the money," she says. "We can go away."
"Where?" I ask her.
"Wherever you say. You can even have women.

Girls your own age. They like to talk to me. I can be of help to you . . ."

"I have a girl," I tell her.

"You'll live—without her."

Joe comes in and says, "I called you—at Amy's. When she wouldn't tell me where you were, I called Marty. Not home yet, he told me," he says, looking at Betty. "It didn't take me long to figure where I'd find you."

"Sit down," I tell him. "You're out of breath."

"Like you were," he says. "The day you came in here."

"What do you want?" Betty asks him.

He stares at me. "I'm leaving *tomorrow*. I want an answer."

"Leaving for where?" Betty demands.

"That's up to Nick."

She stares at him, frightened. "You're crazy," she says.

"We're gonna open up a restaurant," Joe tells her.

"I'll buy him *two* restaurants!"

"*Mine* comes with Amy."

She looks at him in disgust, then turns to me.

"Tell him," she says.

"Tell me what?" Joe asks.

"He doesn't need Amy. I give him all he wants."

"Shut up," I tell her.

She walks up to him, slowly. "In your own house, and you didn't even know it . . ."

"Stop it!" I yell.

"Every night!"

Joe looks at me.

I start to cry.

Letting out a roar, he chokes and collapses.

"Water," he says. "Get me water."

I run to the sink, then take him in my arms. His eyes are bulging, his mouth open. I shake and shake him—as I did my father.

"I'll come with you," I shout. I hug and kiss him.

"Filth!" Betty screams, and comes at me, punching, pounding. I try to shield myself, back to the sink, where I grab her hands and pick up Joe's scissor.

"He's dead!" I cry. "You killed him . . . You killed him . . ."

And that's when I did it. For Joe and for Danny. For Peter and Amy. But mostly for me. Plunged the scissor. Into her mouth. Out. Then in again, her eyes full of wonder.

12

It's easy getting away with murder.

You get on a train.

I tried to say good-bye to Amy, but when I called, the police answered and I hung up.

"It won't be easy killing you," Danny said that night at the party.

Before he finished me, I'd give him chase.

I work on a ranch now. In Colorado. The owner is a widower, the son of a millionaire in glycerine who gave up his home in Chicago with a bowling alley in the basement when he couldn't stop drinking and his wife got cancer.

"You're lucky, Tom," he tells me, almost every

night. "You write. That's like cutting that powder . . . taking that virgin . . ."

He points to the mountain outside his window, the high and clean one untouched by skiers. Drunk, he quotes Hemingway, and passes out.

My name is Tom now. And I've grown a beard. Come February, I'll be going back East.

Once, when we were working, shucking clams side by side, Joe told me about the migrants who live on the river, upstairs, over bars, and how they row out in their dories, scooping up the shad, repairing the nets.

I'll see Amy then, I hope, and tell her I love her, that I wish things were different like that day in the country.

In the meantime, Ricardo's been convicted. And just yesterday, on the news, they reported a mysterious smell in Arkansas, spreading as far north as Kentucky, as far west as Oklahoma.

Has it *all* been a movie? Something Danny dreamed up?

It didn't have to be like this, I'd like to tell Amy. It could have all turned out another way.

Printed in the United States
1755